Novak Grizzly

(Daughters of Beasts, Book 1)

T. S. JOYCE

Novak Grizzly

ISBN-13: 978-1727652871
ISBN-10: 1727652878

First electronic publication: September 2018

T. S. Joyce
www. tsjoyce.com

NOTE FROM THE AUTHOR:

Published in the United States of America

First digital publication: September 2018
First print publication: September 2018

Editing: Corinne DeMaagd
Cover Photography: Wander Aguiar
Cover Model: Travis

DEDICATION

For orange and green M&Ms.

ACKNOWLEDGMENTS

I couldn't write these books without some amazing people behind me. A huge thanks to Corinne DeMaagd, for helping me to polish my books, and for being an amazing and supportive friend. Looking back on our journey here, it makes me smile so big. You are an incredible teammate, C!

Thanks to Travis, the cover model for this book. And thank you to Wander Aguiar and his amazing team for this shot for the cover. You always get the perfect image for what I'm needing.

And last but never least, thank you, awesome reader. You have done more for me and my stories than I can even explain on this teeny page. You found my books, and ran with them, and every share, review, and comment makes release days so incredibly special to me.

1010 is magic and so are you.

ONE

Sometimes, when a heart breaks, it's the most hideous thing in the world.

Being left behind by someone who once promised Remington Novak the moon had destroyed everything she thought about herself, and the way the world worked. She curled her knees up to her chest and traced the raindrops that raced down the window pane.

City bear, living in Sacramento where she didn't belong. Why was she here? Stuck in the middle of this big, busy city, her inner grizzly restless for open spaces. Why had she put herself through this?

For a man.

When she caught her reflection in the rain-spattered window, she didn't recognize herself. Long hair dyed blond for him. She was too thin...for him. She was twelve stories above a street lined with honking cars, in a crowded city, crying...for him. She'd changed everything about herself because that's what she thought being a good mate meant, but she'd been so, sooooo wrong. She'd never been anyone's mate. She'd just thought she was.

Her phone dinged on the cushion of her window seat. For one weak moment, she hoped it was him. She'd been trained to become excited when he messaged. Why? Because he'd become so frugal with his responses she would search for any sign he was still in love with her. So any glowing screen, any ding of a text message, any phone call, her heart had pounded a little faster.

It was Juno, her childhood best friend from Damon's Mountains. Remington tried not to be disappointed, really she did. Juno deserved her attention way more than Kagan ever had, but there was this split second when she wanted to cry. Kagan really didn't care. He'd really left her—the one she'd given up everything for.

Special delivery, Juno had texted. *Clean up all the*

empty ice cream cartons, put a damn bra on, the delivery guy will be there any minute. Call me when you get it.

Remington tossed the cell back onto the cushion and leaned her face against the window. The rain matched her mood.

There was a knock at the apartment door, and she snarled before she could stop herself. All she wanted was to be left alone for a few freaking days. All she wanted was to deal with this heartache the exact way that worked for her, but everyone kept blowing up her phone and pestering her.

"Go away," she called.

"Uuuh, I have a package you have to sign for?" a guy said on the other end of her door.

Aw, for fuck's sake. She didn't want anything. Unless it was another delivery of mint chocolate chip ice cream.

"Leave it at the door!" Remi scrunched up her face and added, "Please and thank you." Even heartbroken, she had some manners.

"You really need to sign for this one, lady. Please, I'm on a time crunch. I'm almost off work, just...help a guy out."

"Fine," she growled. Juno could stuff it; she wasn't putting on a bra.

Remington stomped to the door, threw it open, and held out her hands, barely looking at the startled delivery man. She scratched her name onto the iPad he gave her to sign and then handed it back, one eyebrow arched with impatience. He was in a navy delivery suit with a nametag that read Benny.

"Okay," Benny yelled behind him at the stairwell. "Bring them up!"

"Bring what up?" she asked, panicking slightly.

A half dozen men in firemen suits stomped up her narrow stairwell while an old school boombox started blaring the Catwalk song. "I'm too sexy for my shirt..."

"What the hell?" she asked, stunned as they filed past her, holding vases of bright pink tulips.

"Sorry your ex was such a twat," Benny said. "He was everything that you did not...deserve." He put his hand to his mouth and arched an eyebrow as he murmured, "I'm not so good at rhyming." He cleared his throat and began again, but this time reading off a piece of scribbled notebook paper. "'Kagan couldn't even get your favorite flower right, and now that emotionally constipated little bunion is out of sight.'"

"Did Juno write this?" she asked as the men in her apartment broke out in a saucy round of pelvic thrusting and twerking.

"Yes. 'And so we bid dickhead adieu. He was never right fur you.'" He lifted his voice and pointed to the poem on the paper. "She spelled 'for' like 'fur.' That's pretty funny. Clearly, you're one of those shifters. Your eyes are really freaky."

"That part doesn't rhyme," she called over the pounding music.

"Oh, right." He cleared his throat and read off the paper again. "'Kagan is a fucking asshole, a fucking asshole, a fucking asshole.' I think I was supposed to sing that part, but I'm not a very good singer."

"Fantastic, are we done here?" she called out over the noise, frowning at the gyrating men now removing their shirts.

"Yeah, come on boys." He waved them toward the door. "The lady is declining the full show. Here, this is for you." The delivery guy handed her a sealed envelope.

"I swear to God if this is a glitter bomb," she muttered as she opened it, "I'm gonna maul her."

It was a newspaper clipping. Across the top of it in Juno's handwriting, it read, *Time for a Change, Remi.*

"No need to tip," the delivery guy said as the men all filed out of her apartment. "It's already been taken care of. Have an emotionally stable day!"

Remington stood there in her open doorway, her three-days unwashed hair a mess, wearing her rattiest pajama pants and a tank top with three holes and two teriyaki sauce stains, standing on a pile of take-out menus people kept shoving under her door, and staring at the men who filed down the stairwell and out of sight.

Typical Juno, to make her smile when all she wanted to do was Change and go Godzilla on that... What had she called Kagan? Oh, yeah, emotionally constipated little bunion.

Remington shut the door and made her way back through the maze of tulips the stripper-firemen had boobytrapped her floor with to her little den, aka the nook by her single window where she'd spent the last few days falling apart.

Folding her legs under her, she read the newspaper clipping.

Wanted: A cook/secretary/beer getter/drill sergeant/extra hand for a three-man lumberjack Crew. Pay is decent, hours are long, Crew is rowdy but respectful…mostly. Must be knowledgeable in first aid and not be scared of animals. Must be okay with foul language and dick jokes. Full benefits and a singlewide trailer will be provided. Saturdays off. Must like fun. 1009 Wayward Way, Tillamook, Oregon.

Remington read it again. And again. Her phone rang.

She picked up on the second ring. "Juno, what is this?"

"Tulips," her lippy friend said. "Because Assface kept getting you roses even though you told him three times you don't like roses. That was the first red flag, Remi! He didn't even listen to you. And besides, I'm pretty sure he only got you flowers when he was feeling guilty over something awful he did to you."

"Not the flowers. I mean the newspaper clipping you sent me."

"Oh. That is your new life."

"Uh, no, it's not. I'm not going to go find a job in some fucked-up episode of *Deliverance* with a Crew I don't even know."

"They're a good Crew."

"How do you know that?"

"Because we stalked them!"

"Who is 'we'?" she demanded a little too loud.

"Me, Ashlynn, your dad—"

"My dad researched a Crew. And he's seriously okay with sending me to my demise with a three-man Crew of foul-mouthed, dick-joking lumberjack strangers. I smell bullshit."

"Uh, bullshit must smell like the truth because your dad was the one who sent this newspaper clipping to me."

Remington was dreaming. That's what this was. She had to be dreaming. Her friends and family were not seriously suggesting she pack up her whole life in the city and move out to Tillamook, Oregon to live in a trailer with three strange men. It couldn't be. Couldn't.

Her phone vibrated in her hand right as she opened her mouth to tell Juno she was hanging up. It was a text from Dad. *You should go.*

"Juno, I have to get off the phone. My dad has lost his mind."

"Okay, call me back when you're done. I want to hear what he says."

"Pest."

"I love you love you love you love—"

Remington hung up and typed out a response to her father. *Dad, you know your opinion means the world to me, but this isn't what I should do. I just need some time.* Send.

You need your roots. You do what you want. You always did. I was always proud. You are tough. My tough girl. Always my tough girl. But you need to breathe. Baby Bear. Go there. Find air. Just breathe.

Remington's eyes filled with tears. He was right. She hadn't been able to draw a deep breath since she moved to Sacramento, and her father was a seer. He saw things beyond this world.

So…okay.

If Beaston Novak was telling her she needed to do something…

She had no choice but to listen.

TWO

Kamp was going to kill him. That's all there was to it. He was going to kill his crewmate, Rhett, and be done with his miserable carcass.

He grabbed the tools out from under the seat of the firewood processing machine and hopped out of the cab where his old work boots sunk an inch into the mud.

He was going to kill Rhett, and then he was going to kill his good-for-nothing Alpha and be a free man to just live out his days in the mountains, not talking to anyone.

Everyone was awful. He hated everything.

Why? Because it was forty freakin' degrees outside, and he'd asked Rhett to do one thing—

change out the splitter on the firewood processing machine because the blades were dull. And what had he done? Nothing! As usual.

So he was going to take this splitter and shove it up Rhett's ass. God, he hoped he Changed. He truly hoped he did. He'd wanted to fight that sniveling little weasel shit since he'd come out here three months ago.

His radio was blaring "Eye of the Tiger," but he hadn't bothered to turn it off. He could use the soundtrack for his building rage. He'd had it! Had. It. Three freaking months he'd been asking Rhett to do simple tasks that he could manage way faster than Kamp could. Kamp had the older machine, and lucky fuckin' dog Rhett had the new machine that never needed work. But Kamp was doing the job of three people. Why? Because his damn Alpha sucked at managing a Crew.

And speak of the devil himself… As Kamp stomped toward the temporary trailer park they'd set up, who other than Grim should be there with his chainsaw, ripping the cord?

He looked over at him with narrowed eyes and snarled up his lip. Why? Who the fuck knew! And since he didn't bother to ask what was wrong because he didn't care, Kamp yelled out, "Rhett can't do one fuckin' thing I ask him!" and held up the dull splitter.

Without a word, Grim slid his attention back to the massive tree he was about to chainsaw down and went to work. Typical. Grim was hands down the worst Alpha in existence, and here Kamp was, stuck with the worst Crew, none of whom he could stand.

"Way to care!" he yelled over the roaring of the chainsaw.

He'd handle Rhett his damn self, just like he always did. Maybe he should've been Alpha of this stupid Crew. But nope, nope, that sounded like Hell. He didn't want to lead a Crew, which is why this stuff pissed him off so bad. Grim should've put Rhett in his place and brought him into line immediately, but the Alpha of this Crew was totally checked out. Kamp freaking hated both of them. Hated being here, hated everything.

"Hey, asshole!" Kamp yelled at Rhett's trailer where he was probably still asleep. "You're fired!"

And then he chucked the huge blade through the wall of Rhett's mobile home.

THREE

"Oh, good gravy," Remi said as she kicked off a bramble bush that had clutched onto her ankle like it was trying to escape quicksand.

So far, she was horrifically unimpressed with the set-up of this place. First off, GPS hadn't even been able to find the dang address for the trailer park and with the declaration of "You have arrived" had dumped her in a field that apparently doubled as a parking lot.

Arrived where? The wilderness? She was way up in the mountains, and town was a good fifteen minutes away. Though it reminded her of where she'd grown up in Damon's Mountains, the dilapidated sign with an arrow pointing at the ground that said *Thisa way* was about as helpful as a broom with no bristles. After relieving herself of the desperate bramble, she stumbled and tromped up to that sign, pointed straight down at the toes of her shoes. She wiggled the sign to see if it settled easy to direct her to the left trail leading up or the right trail leading down the mountain, but it didn't budge. Apparently, she was supposed to disappear into the ground like she was freaking Alice, and this was mother-freaking Wonderland.

Okay, she could figure this out. There were two trucks parked in the field and a Bronco parked by the trees as far away from the other two as possible. They looked well taken care of, not rusted out, so these were probably the Crews' rigs. Inhaling deeply, Remington searched for any fresh shifter scent, but found none. Just pine and sap and earth. Which meant these boys were homebodies and probably hadn't went to town in a while.

She couldn't find a place more opposite of the city if she tried. A wave of homesickness took her. Not for her apartment, but for Kagan. Weak, weak, weak. He didn't want her, and she was still pining over him.

Gah, she wished her brother, Weston, was here.

He would have the trailer park figured out in no time. He was an amazing tracker.

"Eeny meeny, miney, mo," she murmured, pointing between the two trails. Both were overgrown but worn. "Up it is." Talking to herself made her feel a little better. She wasn't used to the quiet of the woods yet. It was familiar, like the mountains she grew up in, but she'd been in the city for years. Inside her, the animal was quiet. The restlessness had seeped from her bones with every mile she'd driven into these woods. She still couldn't draw a deep breath, but her neck and shoulders didn't ache as much from the constant tension she carried in them.

But if she was honest with herself, she still wouldn't be here lurking around some strange and unfamiliar woods if Dad hadn't told her to.

Five minutes of hiking uphill later, and she came to a level clearing. Four singlewide mobile homes were lined up. They were small, but looked newer, each with a front porch off the front doors that she faced. The porches had just enough room for a rocking chair. Or a cheap bag chair, like the closest one to her had. There were three discarded blue Bud

Light beer cans on that one, too. Slob.

The camp was quiet, but in the distance, she could hear the rumble of a chainsaw and some big machine. A log cutter of some sort, and whoever was driving was playing "Eye of the Tiger" on full volume. She couldn't help the smile that crept to her face. This place sort of felt like Damon's Mountains, with the evergreens and rivers and mountains and rowdy boys. She could tell they'd be rowdy from the pair of four-wheelers parked under an awning with a bunch of tools scattered about, as though someone was refurbishing them. By the empty whiskey bottles by the front wheel of the big charcoal-colored one. By the game of Cornhole and horseshoes set up off to the side. Again with discarded booze bottles. Slobs and drunks from the looks of it.

"Juno, what have you gotten me into?" she murmured under her breath as she approached the first trailer, feeling a bit like Goldilocks and the Three Bears. This trailer had new pink rose bushes in front and a white plastic lawn chair right in the middle of the landscaping. Weird, but okay. As she passed the porch with the discarded beer cans, the house number next was *1007*. Remi frowned and dragged her attention to the next house number. *1008*.

Couldn't be.

Chills rippled up her arms, and the hair on the back of her neck lifted.

Couldn't.

Be.

Breath shallow, she made her way past the pristine white trailer next. There was no chair on the front porch, no landscaping, but there was a garden gnome wearing sunglasses with his middle finger up and a welcome mat that read *Fuck Off*. Quaint.

The next mobile home appeared to be empty. The single front window was open, and there was nothing on the porch, not even a mat to scrape off muddy boots. There was no skirt around this trailer so she could see the cinderblocks it rested on, as if it had just been brought in recently. *1009.*

"Oh my gosh, oh my gosh," she whispered as she came to stand in front of a cream-colored singlewide with a beige porch and green shutters around the single window behind the rocking chair.

The house numbers were dilapidated and lopsided, barely hanging on by their nails, but easily readable.

Her eyes prickled with tears of disbelief.

1010.

Just like the trailer that had been passed around Damon's Mountains when she was a kid. The magic one that gave sanctuary to so many.

Who were these people?

As if conjured by her thoughts, one of the Crew appeared out of the woods like a ghost. Like a loud, cussing, red-faced, furious, tall-as-an-oak, hot-as-hellfire ghost. He was all chiseled jawline dusted with the perfect amount of dirty blond whiskers, a straight nose that flared slightly with what was probably rage, and an intensity in his pretty bi-colored gold and green eyes. She was pretty sure her mouth plopped open and her ovaries went off like roman candles.

And then that sexy man yanked off a yellow hard hat to expose sandy brown hair cut short. That hat got tossed into the weeds, and in his other glove-cladded hand, he carried a humongous red log-splitting blade like the damn thing weighed nothing. His jaw was clenched, which made it looked as sharp as a runway model's, and he was wearing an open blue flannel shirt over a thin white hotboy tank top. His jeans were covered in dirt and oil spots and had rips at the knees, and his work boots had seen some serious trauma. His bright eyes were focused solely on 1010, and when he snarled up his lip, he looked more beast than human. Now that was a man. They didn't make them like him in the city.

"Hey, asshole!" the man roared at 1010. "You're fired!"

And then the blazing-eyed shifter threw the gigantic blade into the side of the trailer like he was throwing shotput.

The resulting damage to 1010 ripped right out of her any charitable thought she'd had about the man. She hated him before the blade even made contact with the thin siding of the trailer. Remi jumped out of the way as the deafening crash sounded, but the fury over what the man had just done to the trailer...*THE* trailer...pounded through her veins. Pain sizzled through every cell in her body in an instant, and she gritted her teeth as her grizzly shredded its way out of her.

She hit the ground on all fours and was off like lightning to teach that idiot a painful lesson on taking care of important possessions. And 1010 was hella important.

Someone was yelling from the hole in the side of the trailer, distracting the villain, and just as she drew up to him, murder in her heart, the angry man turned.

She saw his lips form the words, *whuuut theee fuuuuuck?* and then she was on him.

She just wanted to kill him a little. Just a little death to avenge 1010. Nothing major.

But the man spun out of the way and Changed in a moment. An enormous lion, nearly the size of her bear, came out of him ready to fight, and they locked onto each other with zero hesitation. A brawler. Good. She would've felt bad killing a pussy cat. But a big old dominant lion? Now, *that* would be way more fun to bleed.

She could hear the yelling from the trailer getting closer, and just as she clamped her teeth on the lion's shoulder, there was a sharp sting on her backside. And another and another. Her rage turned infinite as she released the predator and spun on the new threat.

Some idiot with a paintball gun was shooting her from the hole in the wall of 1010! He gave a warrior cry and did that double-tap move on the trigger and just peppered her with paint and pain.

Well now she was going to have to kill everything! The lion swatted her back legs so hard she fell to her butt and took one ill-aimed pink pellet of paint right in the bear-tit, and now everyone was going to die. Except when she spun to end that stupid lion's life, another equally massive, black-maned lion was brawling with him. She roared because this was her kill and the other lion was ruining everything. But they didn't listen. Then the paintball sniper was laughing like a lunatic and shooting at his own Crew, pink paint splattering against their tawny fur, and this entire Crew was a friggin' disaster. They were fighting each other! No one was even paying attention to her anymore—the big pissed-off grizzly bear.

The black-maned lion swatted the other back a few feet and Changed into a very tall, very muscular, very naked, very tattooed, very scarred-up giant of a man with bright gold eyes and a black mohawk. "Change back!" he yelled, veins popping in his neck.

The first lion roared, but it turned into a man's yell as his body broke back into the sandy-haired man. Beside her, the other idiot tripped and fell out of the hole in the trailer. When his paintball gun went off, he shot Mohawk in the left ass cheek. He clenched hard and turned a terrifying glare onto the clutz lying on his belly in the weeds, his bare feet propped up on the trailer.

"Whoops," the Village Idiot muttered. "Accident."

Remi Changed back, but no one even glanced over at her.

"Seriously?" the sandy-haired man asked Mohawk, standing to his full height. His shoulder was badly clawed, but she couldn't remember if she'd done that or if it was from the lion fight. Red was streaming down his arm. "A grizzly shifter attacks me, and your response is to fight me, too? Some Alpha you are." His words were low and simmered with hot rage. He stood there, staring down his own Alpha, his fists clenched at the sides of his powerful thighs.

Big dick. Remi swallowed hard and blinked but it wasn't a mirage. That man was hung like a damn mammoth. *Look away. Look anywhere but at his dick. Don't get caught. Look at Mohawk.*

She ripped her attention away from the sandy-haired man's nethers just in time to see the Alpha shrugged up one shoulder like he didn't give a rip about the call-out. He bent at the waist and picked up a piece of tattered jeans. "That was my favorite pair." His attention arched to her. "Why are you here?"

"My name is—"

"I know who you are. Why are you *here*?" he repeated.

"I invited her," the sniper muttered from where he was still lying in the grass in his blue plaid boxer shorts, fiddling with his paintball gun.

"What?" the two brawler lions demanded in unison.

"I put out an ad for someone to cook us food because I'm tired of eating chili dogs for every meal, and I thought it would be more fun to have someone else here than hang around with you two dipshits all day. We're supposed to give her a trailer and pay her thirty thousand a year, too. So, you know, get your checkbook out, *Alpha*." The way he said the last word was like a cuss word.

All three of these men hated each other.

Seriously...what had Juno and Dad gotten her into?

"I think I should leave," she gritted out, good and pissed they'd wasted her time and money in travel expenses. "Y'all are a disaster."

The sandy-haired man's gaze landed on her at last, and something changed in his face and demeanor. His eyes were still too bright, but the rigid lines of his face softened for just a moment before he put on a mask of aloofness. "Who are you?" he asked, lifting his chin slightly.

"I'm out of here." She turned and, bare-ass naked, limped past her shredded clothes back toward the trail that would lead her out of there. A little piece of her was irritated these boys were getting a good look at her pink painted ass, but more than anything, she was just disappointed. Not just in the loss of this opportunity, but the destruction of 1010, the horrible timing in having to see that happen, this mess of a Crew, this not being her escape after all. She was disappointed in everyone and everything, her life in general, all of it. This was the last blow she wanted to deal with. It was all too much, too overwhelming. A mountain had rested on her shoulders to begin with and this added rock was one rock too heavy.

The back of her leg hurt so bad, she almost couldn't put weight on it. Stupid lion had got one good slap on her, claws extended. She hoped that injury on his shoulder was her doing.

"Don't leave!" the paintballer yelled. "That was the most fun I've had in weeks! You totally kicked Kamp's ass!"

She rolled her eyes and stepped around a neon green lawn chair someone had left toppled in the yard. Nah, on second thought? She turned and punted it. In her fury, she'd used her bad leg and it hurt like a mother-lover. The chair broke into splinters against a tree, and that, at least, was four percent satisfying.

"What's your name?"

Remi shot a look back over her shoulder. The sandy-haired man was following. Kamp the 1010 Destroyer.

She ignored him and made it to the tree line, but she could still hear him following behind her. She tried to growl, but the bear inside of her wouldn't cooperate. Weird and obnoxious.

"Hey, wait up a sec," Kamp said, pulling her elbow gently.

She spun and shoved him in the chest. "Don't you touch me."

Hands thrown up, he backed off. "You're hurt."

"And naked and annoyed, and I don't want to be

here anymore."

His shoulders lifted with the big gust of wind he inhaled. "Look, it's getting dark. We have an extra trailer with a bed and everything. We're shitty at being a Crew, but we're all good at doctoring."

"And why is that? Because you fight all the time?"

He flashed her a ghost of a smile and covered his dick with his hands, then shook his head at the ground. "Look, none of us want to be here. I get you wanting to go, but I don't feel right watching you leave, bleeding because of me. Let me fix you up, you can get some good sleep tonight, and let me check the bandages in the morning, then you can go. No one will try to stop you."

The rock music cut off suddenly in the distance. He glanced back at the woods and yelled, "Don't touch my machine!" His voice echoed through the mountains.

"I'm changing your splitter blade like you asked, you cock-sucking-thunder-twat!" came the echoing reply.

Remi snorted, but cleared her throat to hide it because Kamp was definitely growling.

His jaw twitched with how hard he was clenching

his teeth. He really did have a model face, and an intensity to his gaze that would buckle most woman at the knees. She was trying to keep her eyes north of the border, but his dick was so big he was having a hard time keeping it all covered up.

"Look," he said, "I can offer you first aid and a chili dog."

"You shouldn't have hurt that trailer," she gritted out softly.

A frown tainted his striking features. "Why do you care?"

"Because the number is 1010. You could've thrown that blade through any other trailer here, but you picked that one. You shouldn't have done that."

His eyes narrowed. "Who are you?"

"Remington Novak."

His face went totally slack, and his lips parted in shock. Oh, he knew who she was all right. Most shifters had that reaction when they heard her last name. Daughter of Beaston, one of the most well-known shifters on the planet. One of the most well-respected. One of the most terrifying if anyone laid a finger on a person he loved. She'd always been under the umbrella of her father's protection, and it intimidated most.

Kamp swallowed hard and cleared his throat, gestured to her leg. "It's bleeding pretty bad. Come on." He twitched his head and turned on his heel. He didn't look back as he walked away, as if he expected her to follow. Normally, she wouldn't follow a man. Normally, she would've flipped him off behind his back, made her way to her truck, and sprayed gravel as she peeled out just to spite his bossy ways. But he was bleeding really bad, too, and hadn't winced or complained, wasn't even favoring it.

"You're hurt, too."

"Not really."

"Is this the part where you're going to lure me into your singlewide and get me to doctor you back? Because I have to tell you, I'm not that kind of girl."

"Good," he called out simply. "I don't like people touching me. You're safe from me."

Remi frowned at his receding silhouette. Well, that was an unexpected answer. And what had he meant about none of them want to be here? Why would they form a Crew then? Crews were usually groups of friends who depended on each other, but these three men didn't fit that bill. A shifter who didn't like touch? Well, that was shocking. Touch was important to their animals. It was a security blanket.

But her dad had told her to come here and breathe. She didn't know what that meant, but maybe it wouldn't hurt to stay the night, just one night, and then she could leave in the morning.

"Light the fires and kick the tires, Novak," Kamp called over his shoulder. "If you bleed out, your dad will skin me alive."

Remi looked down at her throbbing leg. Well, he wasn't wrong. Beaston hadn't gotten that nickname because he was tame. Plus, Kamp had a very appealing hide, she thought, checking out his muscular ass as he made his way to one of the trailers. It would be tragic if he got skinned.

So, she limped along behind him.

One night, no more, and she could get some of her questions answered.

Just one teeny tiny miniscule little night, and then she could get back to her life as a city bear.

FOUR

"That's Rhett," Kamp said in a growly voice as he gestured to the man dragging a pillow, a blue comforter, and a bag of cool ranch potato chips from 1010 to 1009.

He didn't have any tattoos and looked fit as fuck with perfectly spiked hair and a devil-may-care expression. He was more like a model than a logger. Rhett winked at her just before he made his way into 1009.

Kamp huffed a pissed-off sound and dragged his attention back to the first-aid kit he was rifling through on his porch. *Kit* was a bit of an understatement. It was a huge plastic bin with bulk medical supplies.

He'd brought her a pair of ripped-up jean shorts that fell past her knees and had to be belted and a plain blue T-shirt that smelled like laundry detergent and cologne. Not that she was sniffing, but it smelled really good. She couldn't look any frumpier if she tried. Going commando in denim was downright uncomfortable, and her nipples were all perked up thanks to the soft fabric rubbing on them and the cool October breeze.

"Do you use that first-aid kit often?" she asked as she sat down on the single brown lawn chair beside the front door.

"If you were a normie, I'd lie and say 'Nope, it's only for rare occasions.' But you're a Novak, which means you were raised in the Gray Back Crew." His lips twisted in a smirk. "Which means there's no need to pretend monsters don't exist with a girl who was raised by them. I'm guessing you're pretty good at first aid yourself." Locking her up with a bright gaze, he challenged her, "Tell me I'm wrong."

Huh, he really did have bi-colored eyes. The green one stayed nice and steady, and the other changed from gold, to green, and back to gold with his emotions. He was really handsome, kneeling there, a roll of bandages in one hand, clad in only a pair of old jeans and a belt with a bald eagle on the belt buckle. His muscles weren't just for show. He was a worker. She could tell the difference between a gym rat and a man who built his body on work for pay.

"You're not wrong," she murmured. "The Gray Backs have the reputation for being one of the most volatile Crews in the world, right?"

He nodded and opened a water bottle, then positioned the lip of it over her clawed-up leg, a washrag held under the gashes. "That's what I've heard. I was raised on tales of the shifters of Damon's Mountains. My mom followed the Crews like the humans did. Every news story, every article, every post online..."

When he poured the water over the marks, she winced and stared off into the woods. With stuff like this, it was better not to look until it was cleaned and done.

"Tough giiiirl," he murmured. Was that a purr at the end? Just a split second of one? Or had she imagined it?

Next was the bad part. Whatever cleaning solution he used burned like she'd stuck her leg in a fire, but like he'd said, she was a Novak, and Novaks didn't show weakness. So she kept perfectly still and clasped her hands in her lap primly. More water, and then he was bandaging her up with quick, skilled, confident motions. A few strips of purple tape to keep it in place, and she was right as rain. Still hurt, but not as bad.

"I won't touch you," she promised, gesturing to his bleeding shoulder.

Kamp looked at his injury and backed up a couple of steps. And then he poured the bottle of cleaner over his arm without even a grimace. "All done," he murmured. "Don't fuss. You'll waste your time."

"Why?"

"Why what?" he asked, his eyes narrowing.

"Why don't you like touch?"

"Never have. I wasn't a kid who needed a lot of hugs." He stared off into the woods with his arms crossed over his chest, so she supposed he was done with this conversation. Stubborn man. But when she parted her lips to change the subject, he said low, "I had a lady, and she needed touch, and I gave in. I gave in and I started to like it, and I started to crave it, and I started to need it, and it made me weak." He slid a bright eyed glance at her, and then down at the toe of his boots as he finished, “And it hurt worse when she left.”

A wave of ache washed through her chest. She knew all about that feeling. Someone had damaged him, and his reaction was so recognizable. How many times over the past week had she promised herself never to let a man touch her again? To never let another person in so she never had to hurt like this again?

She cleared her throat and gave him an out with a new conversation. “Why did your mom follow my people?”

Leaning back on the porch railing, he shrugged up his bad shoulder. “It was a way to feel connected to something, I guess.”

“What about her Crew?”

“No Crew for us. I tried to find one for us when I was older and having trouble with the animal, but I couldn’t find anyone I wanted to pledge fealty to. And they wanted my mom to Turn. I didn’t know how to be around shifters, and I was dominant, so any Alphas I talked to tried to put me in my place.” A slow smile took his face. “I don’t take orders well. So…my mom raised me on her own. She was interested in shifters because I was one, but she was all human."

"That's okay if she's human. There are humans in Damon's Mountains."

"Was."

"What?"

"She *was* human." Kamp clamped the lid on the first-aid kit with a click and lifted it up like it weighed less than air. "And not every Crew is as accepting as your people. You can take Grim's trailer tonight. He won't be back until the morning."

"I'm sorry. Whatever happened to your mom…I'm sorry for it."

He pursed his lips and gave her a single nod, and then he made his way to the door of his trailer.

"Why won't…Grim?...be back tonight?" she asked, just to make sure she really could stay in the angry Alpha's trailer without waking up dead.

"Because he sleeps in the woods."

"Uuuuh, why does he do that?"

"Because he's an animal," Kamp said, shoving the door open and pausing in the doorway. "We all are."

And when the door swung closed behind him, she startled with the loud sound of the slam. A dozen memories of working in the shop with her dad flashed through her mind. She could fix the door so it wouldn't close so violently. Maybe she would adjust it before she left in the morning. It would probably bother her forever if she looked back on her night at this trailer park and thought about his eternal slamming door.

"Scared yet?" Rhett asked from where he was leaning on the porch of 1009. She hadn't realized he'd come back out. He might've looked like a model who belonged in some big city, but this man could be eerily quiet when he wanted to be. It wasn't often she got snuck up on.

"Nope," she murmured, standing to test weight on her bad leg.

"Well, you should be. This is a last chance Crew. You know what that is?"

"Yes, I do."

He grinned brightly. "A Novak Grizzly. I'll be damned. When I put out that ad, I thought we would get a plaything who would run away from here screaming. Not you. You went griz first thing. Well done. You should challenge yourself and stick around. See how much you can take."

"Nice try, but challenge not accepted."

Rhett narrowed his eyes and nodded, then jogged down the steps and headed for the trail that led to the parking lot. "Just as well." He gave her a little salute. "I'll be back soon, Griz."

"My name is Remington. Where are you going?"

"To get your crap from your car, Griz," he called over his shoulder as he hit the tree line.

"But my keys are in my purse!" she called, standing.

"Then I'll just break the window!"

"Rhett!"

The obnoxious man turned around with a baiting smile and held her keys up in the air.

"Where did you—"

"Stole 'em. Be back in a jiff!"

She didn't know how she felt about him going through her car. He'd proven himself a thief, and she had twenty dollars in the cupholder.

"He probably won't roll your car off the cliff," a throaty, growly voice said.

Grim stood leaning against the trailer with the pink roses. They were the complete opposite of him. The flowers were perfect, down to every last petal.

There were no dead leaves, and from the looks of it, the thorns had been cut off. The roses were delicate and beautiful, a stark contrast to the tattooed, dark-haired giant who stood there glaring at Remington. The other mens' eyes had changed back to their human colors, but not Grim's. They were as bright gold as when he'd been a lion fighting his own Crewmate.

"Why did you answer that ad?" he asked.

Remington shrugged. Honesty was best. Shifters could hear a lie. "I guess I got to the point in my life where I thought, why not?"

"Your dad." He cleared his throat and stood up straighter. "Don't want no problems with him. You can stay the night, but no more."

Before she could change her mind, she asked, "What's wrong with you?"

A slow, wicked smile stretched his face. "Everything."

He turned and walked away, disappeared into the woods like an apparition. Kamp had said to stay in the Alpha's trailer, but she didn't want to impose on anyone. Plus, if she was honest, she would rather stay the night in 1010, missing wall and all. Grim might be an animal who slept in the woods, but she'd slept rough many nights, too. Her choice. Any night she'd felt confused or vulnerable, or just needed space away from her big family, she'd snuck out of her trailer and slept out in the woods or in an old tree house her dad had built when she was a baby. Her older brother Weston used to hang out there with his friends from Damon's mountains, but they were older than her and thought her annoying, so she'd steered clear of the tree house when they'd been there. Sometimes she met up with Juno and Ashlynn from other Crews but, mostly, on those nights, she wanted to be alone. Mom had always said she was like Dad in that way.

1010 could have no walls at all, and she would still prefer to sleep there than in a stranger's den.

She limped over and made her way onto the porch, shoved the door open, and took a deep breath before she stepped inside. The entire living room wall was caved in, the blade still hanging out of it. There was a green couch and a flat screen television on a small TV stand. The kitchen was all white-washed cabinets and a farm sink with wooden countertops. The ceilings sagged a little, and the floors had a spongey feel to them with each step she took, but it really did remind her of the old trailer up in Damon's Mountains. The dilapidated thing had fallen apart years ago, but her brother, Weston, had some of the pieces with his Crew—the shutters from the old 1010, if she remembered right.

The sound of her suitcase and purse hitting the entryway startled her so bad she jumped. Rhett had tossed it up with zero care and was sauntering back to the mobile home next door without a word.

Good golly, the shifters up here were social idiots.

Past the kitchen was a single bedroom, and this was where she dragged her belongings. No point in unpacking, so she unzipped the lid and pulled out some clothes that actually fit. In the small bathroom, she scrubbed off the pink paint from earlier with a dark washrag. She dressed, pulled her long hair into a ponytail, and folded Kamp's clothes neatly. And then she limped back out toward the front door of the trailer because she wanted to put them on his porch chair. A full-length mirror was nailed right next to the door. Of course Rhett was vain enough to put one there if this had been his place, but she wasn't as comfortable with her reflection.

Skin as pale as a ghost, dyed blond hair, raven black eyes like her mother's, and a smattering of dark freckles all over her face and shoulders and chest that no amount of makeup could cover. The rest of her features didn't really matter much. It was impossible to see past all the freckles. She'd worn thick makeup over her freckled skin for Kagan because he was so concerned about appearances when they went out. She'd justified it as making sacrifices for her man because that's what love was—sacrifice. But now she thought perhaps she'd been wrong. She didn't really know what love was, or what it was supposed to be, and she probably never would.

She made her way two trailers down to Kamp's place and set the borrowed clothes on his porch chair. But when a loud clang sounded from inside, followed by a muttered curse word, she stepped closer to the front door to listen.

"No, jackass, you should just stay right here, where you belong, in this fucking prison and leave her alone. Decision made." There was a beat of silence, and then "Fuck! I can't let her just starve tonight. She's hurt. She needs food to start healing up good."

When the front door flung open, Remington gasped and stumbled backward, gasping at the pain of landing wrong on her hurt leg. Kamp stood in the doorway, looking just as shocked as she felt, holding a plate with a grilled cheese sandwich and chips.

He inhaled sharply and shoved the plate at her, dislodging three potato chips that tragically fell to the ground. "Here. I made this for you. I swear I didn't poison it."

Slowly, Remington reached out and took the offered dinner. "I would never accuse you of poisoning it."

With a jerky nod, he said, "Good, because I wouldn't. You're safe. Okay. Goodnight." He stepped back into his house and slammed the door closed.

"Uuuuh, Kamp?"

"Yes?" came his muffled reply.

"I brought back your clothes."

"Leave them on the porch, that's fine."

"Okaaay. Did you make a sandwich for you?"

"No. I made three sandwiches for me."

Oh my God, this man is ridiculous. "Okay, well since you made both of us food, do you want to eat that food together? Instead of both of us eating alone?"

"No. Yes. Nope. Maybe. Probably? Maybe we shouldn't. No. Definitely no."

Remington rolled her eyes heavenward, snatched his clothes off the chair, and then barged into his house.

"Your welcome mat says 'fuck off,' but I'm not very good at minding directions."

Kamp snorted. "Clearly." He scanned the living room and then strode right past her and stacked a bunch of outdoor magazines neatly into a pile. Then he picked up a couple empty glasses off the table and straightened a throw pillow on his leather couch. "Um," he said, frowning at her. "I've never had anyone over."

"Ever?"

"Well, I've only been here for three months and I hate the guys, so..."

"Right. No parties at your place."

"I don't have a table yet. I had plans to make one, but I haven't got around to it yet."

"Here is good," she said, taking a seat on the couch. "Your TV is even bigger than the one in 1010."

Kamp pulled a full plate off the counter and set it

on the coffee table next to hers, then made his way back into the kitchen. He popped the tops on two cold beers and settled down beside her, setting one by her plate and one by his. "You say that weird."

"Say what weird?"

"That house number. You've called that trailer 1010 a few times, but your voice goes all soft when you say it."

"It reminds me of something from back home."

Kamp took a big bite of his sandwich and gestured to hers. "Eat good. Food will help you heal faster. I can make more if you want."

"I thought you only made chili dogs," she teased.

"I only make chili dogs for Rhett because I want that dipshit to get annoyed and leave."

She nearly choked on a chip with her laughter. "You three are the worst Crew in the world."

"Agreed. We're all going to get fired. We can't even come close to hitting our quotas because we hate each other and fight all the time and eventually just quit early. I hate it. It means less income. I'm not used to quitting early, but it's hard to care about the guy beside you when he doesn't care about you."

"You wish it was better?"

Kamp shrugged. “I wish I wasn’t here.” He gave her a sad smile and reached for the remote. “I’ll let you pick the show so long as it’s not some romantic bullshit with a bunch of kissing. Unless it’s porn.”

Remington giggled and took a giant bite of sandwich. “Admission,” she said around the bite. “This is the first time I’ve felt comfortable eating like a pig in front of a guy.”

“Shut it. There’s no way to not eat like a pig when you have a motherfucking grizzly bear inside of you. I call bullshit.”

“No, it’s true! My ex-boyfriend was human. He got super disturbed if I went werebear on a rack of ribs. Especially in front of his friends.”

“Well, his friends sound lame. And he sounds like a boring moron. A boron. You dated a boron. Congratulations, you found one; they are super rare.”

She shoveled another bite into her maw and said around the food, “He wath a little boring.”

“My ex-girlfriend left me for a hyena shifter.”

“Ooooooooh,” she said in sympathy. “Burn. Wait, aren’t they notorious for having teeny tiny little peckers? I’m offended for you.”

“Thank you! Finally, someone gets it. She told me

I wasn't 'sensitive enough to meet her emotional needs.'" He did air quotes with his fingers.

"Your ex sounds...ex-hausting." When he rolled his eyes, she laughed. "Ha, ha, haaaa!" He was smiling, though, so he couldn't hate her pun that much.

"That one," she said with a full mouth, pointing to the TV. "I want to see the scores."

"You watch football?" he asked, looking at her as if he'd found a unicorn or a tricky demon and didn't know which one quite yet.

"I play fantasy football, and my quarterback is on this team. When did your ex leave you for teeny-peeny?"

"Three years ago. I gave up on the fairer sex after that."

"Seriously?"

"Look around, Novak. What am I gonna do? Seduce a girl in town and bring her back to my trailer park with my delinquent Crew?"

"One, my friends call me Remi, not Novak. Every time you say that, I feel like one of your bros. Two, you're hot, and not all girls need a mansion. Some like destructive, mildly psychotic lion shifters with temper problems who put logging blades through houses but also know first aid. Someday, someone is going to stumble into your trailer park and point to you and go, 'That mess right there is all mine.'"

One of his eyes had turned a light gold while the other stayed green, and his face had softened as he'd watched her talk. "Are you a future-teller like Beaston? Are you saying that will happen?"

"Not at all. You are probably screwed, and no girl is going to live up here in the wilderness with you guys." She couldn't control her laughter by the end. He shoved her in the shoulder until she toppled over on the couch and spilled some of her chips.

"God, you're annoying, *Novak*," he said, chuckling. "I'm glad you're leaving tomorrow."

"This is a really good sandwich. Your chef skills are on point. Except it's even yummier with turkey in it."

When Kamp took a swig of beer, Remi really did try not to stare longingly as his Adam's apple bobbed in his muscular throat. His lips were perfectly puckered on the lip of the bottle, and his powerful arms stretched the sleeves of his black T-shirt. He smelled like that cologne she'd sniffed on the shirt she'd borrowed. Kamp was yummy.

Remi followed suit and took a long sip of her cold beer, too. "This is good," she said, studying the label. It was a beer she'd never heard of before called Pen15 Juice. She laughed. "The logo looks like it says penis juice."

Kamp rolled his eyes and shook his head. "That was Rhett's only contribution. He swore he was going to name it something epic. He would make all the labels if he could have three percent of any future profit, so I thought he was actually going to take it seriously. But he put this shit on all the bottles, and now I'm stuck with four batches of penis juice beer. He's an asshole and will get zero percent of all future profits."

"Wait, wait, wait," she said, sitting up straighter. "You brew this?"

"Yep. I used to make moonshine, too, but I got a little arrested."

She snickered and made her way into the kitchen. "A *little* arrested," she murmured, looking around for beer brewing equipment. All she saw was a bowl with trail mix and an empty package next to it. There were about a dozen M&Ms in a little pile on the counter. "If you only like the candies, why do you get trail mix?

Why don't you just get a bag of candy?"

"The candy is the only thing I don't like. I can't really eat chocolate," he explained, coming to lean onto the countertop, beer in hand. "My animal feels sick for a day or two when I eat it. But I stay out for work, and the trail mix a good quick snack that keeps me going for a while. It's my favorite thing to eat. I just have to adjust it a little. It's annoying, but I can't find any trail mix like this without the candies."

"I thought dogs were allergic to chocolate, not big ferocious lions." She ate all the orange ones.

"Apparently, cats can be sensitive, too." He frowned at her as she picked another orange one out of the trail mix and popped it in her mouth. "M&Ms all taste the same so I know those aren't your favorite flavors. Favorite color?"

"Nah, my favorite color is teal. Where I'm from, you eat green ones to make you horny and orange ones for bigger boobs."

He chuckled. "Your boobs are just fine."

She jerked her attention over at him. His cheeks were turning red, and he ducked his gaze as he picked at the label on his beer. "They're perfect," he murmured so softly she almost missed it. "I like your freckles, too. And you don't cover yourself when you Change. I like that you are who you are and you don't water yourself down. That confidence is sexy." He cleared his throat and stood up straight. "And I kinda think it's hot that your grizzly came straight for me today. I don't think many people would have a shot at running you over, Novak. Come on, I'll show you where I brew the beer."

There was this silly breezy sensation in her stomach as he passed her by, heading for the back door on the other side of the kitchen. He called her Novak, but for some reason, she wished he would let his guard down and call her Remi.

"You're wrong," she said as she followed him down the stairs in the back.

"About which part?"

"I watered myself down for someone, I'm not that confident, and I let him run me over."

"Did you?"

"Yep, sure did."

He turned and walked backward. "Then why are you here in one piece? And where is he?"

Huh.

Kamp tinked the neck of his bottle against hers.

"Here's to you cutting dead weight. Congrats. You're free."

She didn't know why that made her blink hard and fight back the burning in her eyes. She didn't know why that windy sensation in her stomach got stronger. She only knew how grateful she was when he turned around and walked away before he could witness her weakness in this moment.

Dead weight.

That's exactly what Kagan had been, and look what she'd been doing? Mourning her freedom. Enough that she'd flown all the way here, rented a car, and drove into these unfamiliar mountains, desperately searching for anything that would take her focus off the ache in her heart.

How many times had Kagan called her to see how she was doing? None. He'd left so easy. Just moved on, while she'd given him all this power by breaking down.

Enough. There would be big changes when she went back to the city tomorrow. It was time to get her life back. To get her pride back.

Right at the edge of the trailer park, there was one of those big sheds that looked like a little barn. It was one of those cheap numbers that were always set up in the parking lots of hardware stores, but this one was a little different. Someone had poured a slab for a concrete foundation, and as she stepped inside, it looked like the walls were covered in metal sheeting. Kamp strode right to the middle of the room and pulled the string of the single hanging lightbulb, illuminating the garage-sized mancave. On the back wall, there were three big metal kegs set up on a metal tube mount positioned over a pair of propane tanks. There were two metal racks with different sized metal containers, tubes, and storage bins. Wooden crates of empty bottles, all boasting that Pen15 Juice logo were stacked neatly on the other wall. There were also plastic containers labeled: h*ops, malt, yeast, corn sugar,* and one called *secret ingredient*. There was also a tall, two-seater table with stacked tasting glasses and a couple of empty beer bottles. There was a stainless-steel sink with a big faucet in the corner.

"This is the coolest brewery I've ever seen."

"Ha. It's nothing special. Just a hobby to keep from killing the other two ass-faces that call this place home."

She giggled and took a seat at the table. "You just called two monster lion shifters ass-faces."

She chugged her beer and then set down the empty. "If you hate it so much here, then why do you stay?"

Instead of answering, Kamp followed suit and finished his drink, then opened a mini fridge and pulled out a jar of pickles. He yanked a bottle of vodka off the top shelf of one of the metal racks and poured shots into the glasses on the table. Then poured pickle juice in two more.

"Pulling out the hard stuff tonight," she pointed out. "Just so you know, I'm not gonna get drunk and sleep with you."

Kamp rolled his eyes. "Just so you know, I'm not the type of man who would ever sleep with a drunk girl. Plus, your dad would kill me slowly if anything happened to you. You're about as safe as you can get."

"Mmm, good answer. I haven't had a pickleback shot since I was in Damon's Mountains."

"What else haven't you done since then?"

"Oh, gosh." She searched her memory. It had been four years since she'd followed Kagan from the town they'd gone to college in and moved to the city. "Rode four-wheelers, climbed a tree, shot-gunned a beer, jumped off Bear Trap Falls, Changed with a whole Crew—"

"Listen to your voice." He sat down across from her at the thin metal table. "You miss it."

"No...no, I..." She frowned. She'd been telling herself she didn't miss it so she could keep her head in the city and not be miserable...but maybe... "I miss parts of it."

"How long since you've been back?"

"I visited my old Crew and family on the holidays, but it's been years since I spent a whole week there. Mostly, when I go back, I'm so busy trying to see everyone that it flies by and I'm leaving again before I know it. What about you? Do you visit your hometown much?"

"Cheers," he said, lifting up his vodka.

Oh, he was a tough one. He'd barely given any information about himself, and here she was, spilling her guts. She could clam up, too. "Cheers," she said. They clinked the bottom of the glasses on the table and then it was bottoms up, followed by the pickle juice chaser.

"You look mad."

"I'm not mad," she said primly.

"Your eyes are all squinty and you look like you just sucked on a lemon."

"Nice weather we're having up here." She arched her eyebrows and leaned back in her chair. Which was backless, so she started to fall, wind-milled her arms, and barely caught herself. He was trying to hide a smile but not very well, the oaf.

He looked up at the ceiling and back at her. "This place is a share. No one has been in here but Rhett, and then it was only to ruin my empty bottles."

"You're territorial?"

"My lion is. You were in my den, too. That was a share."

"What happened to your mom? How did she die?"

"Who said she was dead?"

"You did. You said she *was* human."

"And now she's a lion."

Relief washed through her, and her shoulders sagged with her heaved sigh. "Oh, thank God."

Kamp's face was perfectly stoic. "If you talked to her, you wouldn't be thanking God."

"What do you mean?"

"Me Turning her wasn't a purposeful thing, and

the lioness didn't take well. Beer or shot?"

That was terrible. Tragic. He'd Turned his own mom. Had it ruined her? Had *he* ruined her?

"Why are you here, Kamp?"

He snarled up his lip, and one of his eyes turned gold while the other stayed green. When he leaned back in his seat, it creaked under his shifting weight. Crossing his arms over his chest, he glared at her. "You know what a Last Chance Crew is?"

"I've heard of them, yes."

He twitched his chin toward the open door. "Well, now you've met one. We don't fit anywhere else, and we aren't safe to the public if we're rogue. The three of us will kill each other up here eventually. These mountains are a graveyard, Novak. This is where we've come to die."

Her stomach curdled. "That's ridiculous."

"What?"

"That's a ridiculous thing to say. You're fine. You all are."

Kamp huffed a humorless sound. "If you only knew."

"I know enough. I know crazy, Kamp, and you ain't it. Neither is Grim, and neither is Rhett."

"You're gonna make that judgement after knowing us for a few hours?"

"Yep," she said, standing. She made her way to the door. "Maybe you could've convinced someone else you were unsalvageable, but not me."

"And why's that?"

She paused, leaned her cheek on the open door frame, and smiled. "Because I'm the daughter of Beaston. Everyone is salvageable. Especially you. Goodnight, Kamp."

And as she walked away, she heard him murmur, "Goodnight, Remi."

FIVE

A deep, deafening, terrifying noise woke Remi from her sleep.

She'd been sleeping better and harder than she had in weeks, but she shot up in bed when a second, long roar shook the trailer. Something was wrong. She could feel it in the air—the tension, the rage.

She kicked off the covers and bolted for the bedroom door just as the third roar vibrated through the floor, through her feet, up to her shin bones and knees, and struck her right in the heart. This was a roar of anger and infinite pain. The kind that lifted chills on her arms and made her stomach curdle. The floorboards of 1010 were striped with blue moonlight that sifted in through the cheap, open blinds on the windows. Remi sprinted for the front door just as another lion answered the first's call from miles away.

"Shhhit," she heard Rhett say from near the firepit in front of Kamp's trailer. Façade dropped, the jokester was pacing tightly, holding his hands over his ears.

"Rhett?" she asked over another roar. "What's happening?"

"Same shit," he answered. "Same shit, different day. Hate it here. Hate it here." When he lifted his eyes to her, they reflected oddly in the dim porch light—like an animals. They were blue as ice, and he looked...tortured.

"He's bringing in the monster again. He can't fuckin' help himself."

Another roar sounded from inside Kamp's house.

"Oh no," Remi whispered. "He Changed in his trailer?"

"Don't worry, Princess Werebear, he won't be in there for long." An answering roar sounded, much closer now than it had been. "The Grim Reaper is coming."

"The Grim Reaper?"

Rhett looked like he wanted to puke. He gave her a shaky smile. "That's his name. That's our Alpha. The Grim fuckin' Reaper. And your man's calling the beast. Again."

Her man? "But they fought earlier!" she yelled over the roaring, jogging toward Rhett. "They were in control."

"That was Grim during the day. He turns into the Reaper at night. You should get back inside."

"What are you going to do?"

Rhett shook his head and swallowed hard, eyes shining brightly. He lifted his shirt and showed her the deep scars over his ribs, crisscrossing in different shades of red, different stages of healing. "I'm gonna do what I always do. I'm gonna stop them from killing each other. They won't remember in the morning. This is my real job in the Crew—keep them from putting each other down too soon."

Horrified, she asked, "Why are they doing this?"

"They can't help themselves. Grim just doesn't give a fuck, but Kamp? He has a glitch. At night he goes to sleep and dreams of the day he lost someone, and then he wakes up Changed and needing a fight. And the Reaper is always ready. Little by little, they're killing each other. It'll be just me up here soon. You should go inside, Novak. Seriously."

The roaring was constant now, getting closer and closer.

The door to Kamp's trailer creaked as he pushed it open with his massive head. He didn't even look at her or at Rhett. His glowing gold and green eyes were on the woods. Gads, he was enormous. Tawny coat and full mane only a few shades darker. His body was pure power, his muscles flexing with every step he took down the stairs. He trotted toward the edge of the clearing, and there was the Reaper.

"Who did Kamp lose?"

"Novak, get inside," Rhett gritted out, pulling his shirt off as he jogged toward the impending fight.

"Rhett! Who?" she yelled, because it mattered. Kamp's mindset mattered in fights like these.

"His cub!" Rhett yelled without turning around. A massive white lion ripped out of him just as the other two titans charged each other at full speed. And now it was a trio of powerhouse big cat predator shifters about to clash.

His cub?

Kamp had lost his cub?

Tears burned her eyes as everything clicked into place. That's why he was with a last chance Crew. This was something he couldn't recover from. He was hurting. So fights like these weren't just a challenge to take up time and ease the ache. They were a shot at an honorable death.

"Fuck," she whispered, pulling off her sleep shirt. The weeds prickled and poked her tender city feet as she bolted toward the fight. Grim and Kamp slammed into each other like two colliding cannonballs. The force of their impact hit her with a wave of energy that knocked her to the side. Arms pumping, legs burning, she let the bear have her. Big, silver bear, just like her father's, and she had a shot at keeping more scars off Rhett's ribs, had a shot at breaking up the fight, had a shot at saving Kamp...at least for one more day.

She landed hard on all fours and dug into the dirt with her long claws as she pushed her body faster. She was quick in this one, able to run down just about anything, but the three seconds it took her to reach the lion fight were the longest of her life.

Kamp and Grim were fighting to the death. She could see it in their eyes, in the way they sank their teeth into each other and wouldn't let go. They spun and countered so fast they were a blur, and all she could do was run right through them and try to shock them out of the blood lust.

Rhett took a massive swat to his body and went flying a few steps before she reached them. Smelled like blood already. She didn't slow down, just ran right into them and slapped Grim off Kamp. He snarled as he slid in the dirt, claws extended as he tried to get traction. His face was so scarred up, like his whole life had been forged in violence.

Kamp tried to get around her, but she clipped his legs just as he went to charge the Alpha. They were desperately clawing their ways back to each other, as if she wasn't even there.

Enough! Remi let off a roar as long and as loud as she could, right in their faces. She let it rattle their ears. They dropped down to the dirt on their bellies and winced. She glared at the Reaper. *I fuckin' dare you to charge me.*

He was thinking about it, too. He stood, as if he didn't care about dying at all and took a step toward her, then another. The low snarl in Rhett's throat was constant as he came to stand beside Remi, facing the

Reaper with her. Grim looked back and forth between them with such hatred it made Remi's stomach hurt. And then he sat down and began licking his paw like he didn't give a single shit about any of this.

Nice try, Monster. She'd been born a Gray Back. She'd seen that move before. He still cared about the fight, and the second they gave him their back, he'd go for their exposed spines. Remi stood on her hind legs and roared at him again. She landed hard on her front paws and huffed breath, shaking her head, exposing her teeth. *Piss off, Grim.*

He snarled up the side of his mouth, showing her his long, curved canine, and then he stood and sauntered off slowly, giving her his back in a show of utter disrespect. That was him saying she wasn't a threat.

There was this little instinct telling her to chase him down and punish him, but that was just the predator in her. She had good control. Unlike this Crew.

They were the biggest fucking mess.

Behind her, Kamp wasn't there anymore. She looked back just in time to see him in human form take his porch stairs two at a time and slam the door behind him.

Rhett the white lion looked completely defeated and tired of everything. He was panting, staring at her with empty blue eyes, and when he turned and stalked off toward his trailer, there was a new set of claw marks on his ribs. Why did he do that? Why did he only give them a shot at that side of his body?

She wanted to cry for these broken boys. These sick boys. What did they have? No comradery, no motivation to work together, no future. This was no real Crew.

She embraced the pain of Changing back so she could check on Kamp. She stooped and grabbed her sleep shirt on the way to his trailer and pulled it over her wild hair. She felt like Hell. Two Changes in one day, two fights in one day, and she wasn't conditioned for this—not anymore. City bear. These boys would toughen her up quick if she decided to stay. She couldn't, though. This wasn't her fight. She had to deal with the life she'd run away from in the city.

She pulled open Kamp's door and made her way inside. All the lights were turned off, but she could see well enough. He was sitting on the couch with his head in his hands, body humming with tension, every muscle rigid.

She hesitated for only a moment, and then she sighed and sat next to him. He didn't say anything so neither did she. She just wrapped her arms around his middle, hugged him, and rested her cheek on his shoulder.

As minutes passed, he stayed just as tense, not relaxing a single muscle. But eventually, he dragged his hands down his face and shook his head. He smelled like blood, but she already knew him well enough to realize he wouldn't let her doctor him.

"Don't like touch," he murmured.

"Yeah, I don't care."

"He ain't dead."

"Who?"

"My boy. I heard Rhett tell you. Don't you go pitying me. His momma took him. I found out she had a man on the side, and I lost my shit. My mom came over and tried to settle me down, and I bit her when she got too close. The day my mom got Turned, Sophia saw it all. She saw my mom's first Change, and she was already checked out on me. She got scared I would Turn her too, and took my son in the night. She felt safer with her other man. Our cub was just a baby, and now my boy is being raised by some fuckin' hyena shifter. I can't even see him. Can't talk to him on the phone, nothing."

"How old is he?"

"Raider is four."

Four years. Kamp was missing those bonding years a little shifter needed with his father. Remi murmured, "He'll be Changing for the first time soon if he hasn't already."

"He had his first Change six months ago. My mom gets updates from Sophia a couple times a year. If I had any question about the cub being mine before, it was laid to rest with this." Kamp pulled his phone off the coffee table and showed her the lock screen. Little lion cub looking right at the camera, one gold eye, one green. A mini Kamp."

A lump formed in her throat, making it hard to breathe. "Oh, Kamp, he's precious."

"Little brawler. Already got in trouble at preschool for fighting."

"You have rights to see him, you know."

"What rights? Shifter rights? Sophia is human. She's used it to her advantage. Humans always get what they want. The one loophole I had was that shifter cubs needed so many hours with an adult shifter in their life to keep their animal in training. She took that away by shacking up with the hyena, and now I don't matter. I'm allowed to pay child support into a fund for him, and that's the closest contact I'll ever have. I'm not necessary." He swallowed audibly and repeated that last part softly. "I'm not necessary."

And it was those three words that changed the direction of her life.

Kamp was warm under her touch. He was allowing her to hold him, to comfort him, but how long would he be here if things didn't change? His existence on this earth felt very important for reasons she didn't fully understand. Sure, she could go back to the city and rebuild her life there. She could take the break-up as a challenge and make a better life, because that was the best revenge on anyone—be okay anyway. But that determination to get herself living again wouldn't mean a hill of beans if this man, Kamp, wasn't living again with her.

"We're gonna get better together," she murmured.

Kamp huffed a soft laugh. "Yeah, okay." He didn't sound like he believed her in any way, but he would see.

Eventually…he would see.

He didn't know her very well yet, but he would. She was a Novak, and it was ingrained in her to heed her sensitive instincts and fix the things that were broken.

And this broken boy felt special. How did a man become so important after one day?

She laid a tiny kiss on his shoulder, and for the first time since she'd wrapped her arms around him, he relaxed, if just a little.

And with a hardened man like Kamp, any progress was a victory.

So when he leaned over and rested his cheek against the top of her head, she wanted to cry. How long had it been since he'd let himself give into touch and return it?

Another victory.

She would tally them up, one by one, until the day he stopped calling the Reaper.

SIX

It was right before dawn when the mountains were still sleeping and the stars were still out. It was dark in Kamp's living room, but she didn't need to see anything. All that mattered was what she felt—his arms around her.

It had been so long since she'd felt safe. She didn't mean physically. She was a bear shifter and could take care of herself, but how long had it been since she could felt she could lay in a man's arms and not get hurt by him?

She laid there, trying to piece together what made Kamp so special to her. Inside, her bear was fast asleep and quiet. She was at peace, which was ironic considering this entire Crew was at constant war with each other.

Kamp's arm was draped over her hip on the couch, and his forehead rested against the back of her head while he slept.

She didn't want to go. She didn't want to leave this.

That realization hit her right in the gut. Was it possible to feel homesick for a place that wasn't home?

As he inhaled and stretched his legs against the back of hers, those little flutters in her stomach kicked up again, and she smiled in the dark. Big strong, closed-off lion shifter had her all scooped up and was now hugging her tighter in his sleep. That's when a woman knew a man liked her—when he hugged her in his sleep.

She wiggled her bottom against him and snuggled closer under the blanket he'd pulled off the back of the couch and draped over them. It was chilly in the trailer, but she was nice and toasty warm against Kamp the Furnace.

Outside there was a chorus of crickets and frogs, still active in the month before it became really cold.

She felt...peace.

And thinking about leaving here made a little hole in her chest that she was afraid she wouldn't be able to fill up again.

Kamp's fingers gripped her hip, and he rolled against her with a soft, gravelly rumble in his throat. Oh, dear goodness, he was sexy as sin.

His erection thickened and got harder and harder as he pressed it against her backbone. He eased off and then repeated. Hungry man must've been a morning person. She rocked with him, slid her arm back and around his neck to keep him close. A soft groan emanated from him, and her stomach clenched with need.

They moved together faster, and when his lips touched the sensitive spot right beneath her ear, she became lost and let off a long moan. "Please," she begged.

Kamp's fingertips trailed across her hip and then down to the hem of her shirt. He pulled it up and cupped her sex. It felt so good to have him touching her. And if this was the last time she ever saw him, she wanted to actually feel like she was living tonight. He slid two fingers inside her just as he bit down on the side of her neck gently and, oh, she was gone.

Eyes closed to the world as he moved with her, hitting her just right when his fingers went deep. Over and over, faster, as she moved her hips and helpless sounds escaped her. There was a rattle against her back, but it wasn't a growl. It was a satisfied sound that revved her up even more.

Her body tingled for release as he pulled her harder against his dick with each stroke.

"Fffffuck," he murmured, shoving his pants down his thighs.

"Kamp, right there," she whispered desperately as she pressed his hand tighter between her legs.

He bucked fast and hard now, so thick against her back, until suddenly her body shattered around his fingers. When she cried out in ecstasy, Kamp pulled her tightly into his chest. Against her back, his dick throbbed, and warmth spread over her skin in waves as he gritted out her name.

They moved against each other until they were both sated. Until every aftershock was done. Until they were both limp, breath matching each other as he hugged her up tight on the couch.

She didn't want to get up, didn't want to clean up, didn't want his finger out of her. And he seemed to feel the same because they stayed just like that, all warm and safe and happy, silent in the dark.

And Kamp, the untouchable man, let her in a little more. "I like being around you," he whispered.

She smiled and snuggled back into his arms, nestled her cheek against his arm. "I like being around you, too."

Victory.

SEVEN

As she walked away from the trailer park, Remi only looked back once. It's all she would allow herself. The first gray and orange dawn light was streaking across the horizon, and everything was serene. This was probably the witching hour for this Crew, the only moments of peace this place knew.

Her gaze stayed glued on Kamp's trailer, and such a feeling of emptiness washed over her. Why? She'd gotten the break she needed here, and her bear was happy and calm inside of her. She'd felt happy in a time of turmoil. So why did looking at his trailer make her feel like a wrecking ball had made a huge hole right through her?

Maybe she would come back and tell Kamp in

person. Maybe if she could fix his life, she would be brave and come back, tell him face-to-face. If she could pull this off, she wanted to be there for that smile. And she was a believer in good things happening to good people with enough effort. If she believed it enough, worked long enough, it would happen.

She gripped the handle of her suitcase and made herself turn away, made herself walk through the tree line and down the trail with no more looking back. Why did she feel like crying? She was doing something good for someone. She should feel fulfilled, not sad.

The second she cleared the trail into the parking lot, it was obvious her rental car wasn't going anywhere. The two tires on the right side were totally flat.

In ripped-up jeans and a stained, threadbare Bud Light T-shirt, Rhett leaned against a tree. He wore a smirk on his face. "Whoops," he said in a voice that said he wasn't remorseful even a little bit.

Remi stomped over to the car and ran her fingers over the slash marks in the tire. "Why did you do this?" she asked.

"That's like asking a beaver why it chews wood. Because I fucking wanted to."

"But why?" she asked louder, rounding on him.

Rhett shrugged and looked bored.

Self, don't kill him. You'd look awful in prison-suit orange.

Remi breathed out slowly to calm the boiling rage in her blood, and then she made her way over to the white jacked-up Chevy on the edge of the trees.

"What are you doing?" Rhett asked.

Yep, that told her this was definitely his truck and not Kamp or Grim's.

"You have one day to return that rental car to the airport," she called, running her fingers under the front right wheel well.

"Or else what?"

"Or you'll have Beaston up here doing it."

A snarl sounded, but she ignored it. No spare keys in the wheel wells of the left-hand tires either. Remi hoisted her suitcase into the bed and yanked open the door, got in, and then slammed it closed beside her. Then locked it. "Keys, keys, where are them keeeeeeys," she sang softly as she searched the glove compartment and the cupholders.

"They aren't in there!" Rhett called out.

But when she pulled down the driver's side sun visor, a pair fell out.

"Shit," he muttered from right outside the window. Attached to the keyring was a small musical instrument. "Is this a rape whistle?"

"These are very dangerous times!" he yelled, jingling the locked door. "Get out of my truck."

"Shouldn't have slashed my tires, Rhett." She turned on the truck and revved the engine, smiling grandly at him through the window. "Bye bye now."

"No, no, no, no, no!" he said in quick succession as she pulled a wide circle toward the road that would lead her down the mountain and into town. And as she picked her way to the mouth of the road, she heard him admit something that made the emptiness inside her even bigger.

"I wanted you to stay!"

EIGHT

Kamp eased one eye open. There was a single sunray beaming him in the eyeball. Stupid sun. Wait...sunlight?

He sat upright and scrambled to check the time on his phone. 8:03 am.

"Oh, shit!" he croaked, bolting from his couch bed. "Remi? Why didn't you wake me?" he asked, sprinting to the bedroom. The bathroom light was on, but as he skidded past, no one was in there. Wait, hold up...what?

He shoved the door open wide and searched the small bathroom. She really wasn't in there. "Remi?"

No answer.

"Remington!" he called out as he searched the

bedroom next. "Novak!"

No answer.

She probably went back to 1010 to shower or something.

Frown hurting his face, he made his way outside and to 1010, but he could tell right away she wasn't in there. The trailer park just felt…empty.

"What the hell?" he murmured as he made his way back into his mobile home. She hadn't even said goodbye. Wait…there was a folded piece of journal paper on the coffee table near his phone.

The stiff paper crinkled as he unfolded it.

Dear Kamp,

You weren't anything I expected, but you were the best surprise. Lunch is in the fridge. Work hard today. Finish your shift. Feel good about the accomplishment, even if you don't think it's a big deal. Last night was fun, and I'll never forget it. For a lot of reasons. Don't forget me either.

Remi

p.s. You made me happy for a little while. That is a

big deal to me. Thank you.

A goodbye letter? Full of disappointment, Kamp crumpled the letter and chucked it at the wall. He didn't do this. He didn't sleep with random women. It wasn't a relief to him that she'd done her leaving without him making her breakfast and staring at her pretty freckles for a few more minutes. He wasn't ready to be left. Again. Wasn't ready to be separated from her. He wanted more time!

"Fuck!" he yelled, his insides sagging with regret.

Kamp scrubbed his hands over his hair and then made his way to the wadded-up letter. He stared at it for a three-count and then stooped, picked it up, unfolded it, and read it again. He'd made her happy for a little while, and now she was gone.

"Fuck," he repeated in a softer voice.

He folded it back, careful to keep the creases just the same as she had made, and set it on the kitchen counter right next to a glass jar of trail mix. He popped open the lid, but he already knew what he would find. Inside, there were individual sandwich baggies of snacks, and the M&Ms had all been removed, leaving only the parts he liked. It meant more than she would ever know that she'd taken care of this small thing. In the fridge, there was a Tupperware container with a sandwich stacked high with meat, spinach, and tomatoes and a nectarine on the side. Beside that was a baggie of green olives and a bottled water.

Kamp huffed a breath and gripped the handle to the fridge door tighter. No one had made him a lunch since...well...he didn't even know when someone had cared that much.

His mind on her like a satellite circling, he showered and got ready for work. Grim wouldn't care if he was late. He didn't even care if he showed up or not, and Rhett was probably sleeping in, too. They were all going to get fired, but today was going to be different. Why? Because she'd told him to make it different by finishing the shift. And he owed her. For one entire night, he'd felt normal. He'd felt okay. He'd felt accepted and unbroken. And that was a gift. Remi hadn't even realized the present she'd given him. For one entire night, he'd had a break from his own head.

Sack lunch and snacks in hand, Kamp made his way outside and up the hill. He didn't make it a hundred yards before Rhett sauntered out of the woods like a creepy stalker and started walking beside him.

Kamp narrowed his eyes at Rhett. The trail was too small for them to both walk side-by-side like this, and they were both hitting trees. "Piss off."

"I slashed her tires." Rhett said it so calmly Kamp didn't know how to react. "I slashed them and she still left, and everything is horrible. We can't keep anything nice. I hate this Crew." And then the psychopath walked off into the woods toward his log cutter, pulling his yellow hard hat on as he went.

Well, Rhett was right for the first time ever—everything was horrible.

Now he got to miss his kid and the girl who got away, because that's what Remi was. She was special. He felt it down to his bones, but he was here, and he couldn't make her stay for more than one night. Fuck everything.

He climbed into his machine and turned the engine. It caught. Hallelujah, it was a miracle.

Finish your shift.

Okay, he would. He didn't even care what Grim and Rhett accomplished today. He wanted to make Remi proud, even if she never knew.

NINE

Kamp's ex-girlfriend was good at hiding.

All Remi had to go on was a first name, and she'd just spent three hours online searching for anything on her. The woman didn't even have social media unless she went by a different name now.

Blowing out an explosive breath of frustration, she connected the call she'd been putting off.

"Hey, String Bean," her brother, Weston, answered.

Remi grinned, "Hey, Gym Rat."

Weston snorted. "You wouldn't call me that anymore if you saw me right now. I've been working myself to the damn bone."

"So you look emaciated now? I call bullshit."

"Atta girl, call bullshit on everything. When are you coming up to visit? You know the whole Crew would love to see you."

"Ha, I'm nowhere close. I'm actually staying at a little one-star hotel outside of Tillamook, Oregon right now, and I'm about to beg a favor, so prepare yourself."

"What do I get in exchange."

"Extreme gratitude from your baby sister?"

"Boring. I want those yams you make at holidays. The buttery cinnamon ones? Ship that shit, I have a craving."

"Typical Weston, thinking with your stomach."

"Who do you want me to track?"

"Ha. You already know why I called."

"Yup."

"I've got a first name only. Sophia. She's human and paired up with a hyena shifter. Has a little lion cub about four years old named Raider."

"Hmm," he grunted thoughtfully. "What's this to you?"

Remi shrugged like he could see her through the phone. "Peace, I guess. A way to do something good for someone with no strings attached."

"You okay, sis?" he asked in a somber tone.

"No, but I will be."

"Kagan was a piece of shit who didn't deserve you. You know that, right? You protected him and hid all the bad parts, but all those changes in you? The changes you made for him? Find a man who likes you just how you are."

"And what if I don't even know who I am anymore?"

"Then figure out a way to get back to that girl, Remi. And then let someone love you who actually deserves your time."

"Easier said than done. I don't even know how to find my old self."

"Step one…do something good for someone with no strings attached."

There was a smile in his voice as he repeated her words, and she swallowed hard before she responded so he wouldn't hear how choked up she was. "Tell Avery hi for me."

"Okay, I will. Tell Kamp hi for me."

A shocked sound bubbled up from her throat, but Weston only laughed and hung up the phone. Mother trucker. What did it mean that Weston knew his name? Her brother had the sight like her dad, but how did he know about Kamp? Had it been gossip in Damon's Mountains that gave him knowledge on the lion Crew? Or was it one of his visions? The answer to that mattered, but when she texted him to ask, he didn't respond. Nor did he pick up his phone when she tried to call back.

Double mother trucker.

Feeling grumpy and confused, she sat in that hotel watching talk show reruns until her phone lit up an hour later with a response from Weston. Finally. But when she checked the message, it didn't address her questions about Kamp. It only said:

Sophia Nailor, human, married and mated to Todd Nailor, Hyena shifter.

Works at Daisy Dukes Flower Shop

14568 Harris St, Eugene, OR

Huh.

That was only about a hundred-fifty miles from here as the crow flew. Sophia wasn't far. Did Kamp realize his son was so close?

She thanked her brother and grabbed her lucky

hoodie, shoved her feet into her old, worn-out hiking boots, and made her way out the hotel door and to Rhett's truck. He was going to have to wait a bit to get it back. She searched herself for a single ounce of guilt over her grand theft auto, but found none.

She used the GPS on her phone and drove an hour through beautiful mountains before she pulled over for gas. When she checked the time on her phone while she stood at the pump, there was an unknown caller who had texted.

Hey, Novak. The trailer park is lame without you. I finished a shift, but no one was here to give me a round of applause, so I'm in the trailer with a TV dinner, a cold beer, and some candy-less trail mix this cute girl I know made. Thanks for taking care of me today. Just so you know, you're a really cool girl, and last night wasn't just a hookup. At least it wasn't for me. I'm glad Rhett tricked you into coming out here for a day. Also, I turned your car into the rental place after work. No late charges. Keep Rhett's truck as long as you want. Asshole deserves it, ha. Good luck with everything.

p.s. you made me happy for a little while too.

- Kamp

While she was reading it a second time, the gas nozzle clicked loudly to tell her the truck was full and startled her. When she looked up, she caught her reflection in the window of Rhett's truck. For a split second, there was a spark of recognition. She wasn't so pale and sad looking. She wore a soft smile, and her eyes weren't tight at the corners. Such a change because of a message from a handsome stranger. Stranger? Hmm, that word didn't feel right. They'd had something last night, something she didn't understand. Something that made her miss him already. Something that made her want to take care of him because she had a feeling he would be really good at taking care of her back.

Broken lion, but he didn't feel broken to her. He felt...familiar, like her heart recognized his heart.

God, listen to her mushy thoughts. She was losing her mind.

Remi was the only one at the dusty old gas station right now. It was a small one-horse-town, self-serve type of place with a barbecue joint attached to the side. A man in a navy apron was standing next to a billowing smoker, checking the temperature on what looked and smelled like a delicious slab of brisket. When she inhaled deeply, her stomach growled. She'd skipped lunch, and it was about dinner time. She would've given just about anything to be sitting in Kamp's living room right now eating a TV dinner with him, but barbecue was a fair enough substitution.

She replaced the gas cap and jogged across the parking lot. There was a little girl in a pink sundress and rainbow tights scribbling on the sidewalk with blue chalk. She had drawn a sun, flowers, and then a bunch of numbers in a row. 32101023. The numbers that stuck out the most were the middle ones. 1010. She came to a stop, and a smile stretched her face as the little girl looked up.

"Hi," she said, waving her chalk.

"Hello," Remi said.

"She's learning her numbers in pre-school and wanted to practice out here," the pit boss explained as he closed the metal lid of the old smoker.

"Practice will make perfect," she said, unable to take her eyes from those numbers. She hadn't noticed that number in years, not once in the city. Now it was everywhere, on the trailer and here, just as she was headed to find Kamp's son.

What did it mean? Felt like a good omen.

"You okay, lady?" the man asked, his head canted as he squinted against the sun to look at her.

"Yeah." She nodded once. "I'm okay. Hungry, but okay."

He chuckled and twitched his head toward the back. "We have the best barbecue sandwiches in Oregon."

Her mouth watered just thinking about it. Inside, the hole in the wall restaurant reminded her of a place back in Damon's Mountains. Moosey's Bait and BBQ. The similarities made her smile stretch so big her face ached. These mountains were something else.

She ordered a sandwich, chips, and a bottled orange soda. She popped the top with a bear paw bottle opener keychain Weston had given her for her last birthday, and she took a seat at a picnic table in the corner of the room. She opened up her phone to read Kamp's text again, but there was a new one that dropped her heart right down to her toes. It was from Kagan. It was a picture of a bouquet of roses in a glass vase sitting outside her apartment door.

I brought you a special delivery today but you weren't home. And Juno said something about you moving on? I think I misunderstood her. We need to talk. I made a mistake. I miss you. Where are you?

She exited the text in a rush and dropped the phone like a hot potato. She stared at the wood grain of the table, her mind racing. She'd wanted him to show up and take it all back so badly. How many times in the last week had she imagined him fixing what he'd done? But instead of rejoicing, that text gave her this sick, empty feeling. Reading his words and seeing the roses he brought made her stomach curl in on itself, so she wrapped her arms around her middle to ease the uncomfortable feeling.

Something inside of her was different—in a good way. Kagan had never brought about a positive change in her. One day with Kamp, and she felt like she was on the right track to finding a part of herself she really missed.

She typed out her response in a rush. *I'm more of a tulip girl. You can't just leave and come back whenever it's convenient for you. I made a mistake, too. It was you. Please lose my number.*

She pushed send before she could change her mind because she didn't want to be that weak girl she'd been at the end of their relationship. She'd let him step on her too much, change her, just to try to make them work. But that wasn't love. A man couldn't stay the same and ask his lady to mold herself into the perfect shape to fit him. They had to just...fit.

Her food came up, but her chest felt all tight and she'd lost her appetite. Her head hurt from all the swirling thoughts and confusion, and with trembling fingers, she texted Kamp back. *My ex just sent me a message.*

Thirty seconds later, her phone rang.

She picked up on the first ring, a flutter of excitement in her chest.

"You want to talk?" Kamp asked.

"Not really about him. I told him to lose my number. It's just still a little new. And it was a bad breakup."

"Want me to kill him?"

She huffed a laugh and then exhaled in relief as the tightness in her chest eased. "I know you're joking."

"Am I?" he asked. His voice did sound a little growly.

"Jealous already?"

"Jealous? No. But I'm not a fan of anyone messing with your head. Are you back in the city?"

Pursing her lips, Remi looked around the barbecue joint and answered, "Not yet, but soon."

"Mmm." His voice was all deep and rumbly and sexy. "I can't stop thinking about your pussy."

Remi nearly choked on air, and her cheeks blazed with fiery heat as she whispered, "Kamp!"

"I'm serious. My biggest regret in life is that I didn't taste you."

"Oh, my gosh," she whispered, her eyes bugging out of her head. This was dirty talk. This was happening. To her. It was happening to her!

"You…would…want to…"

"Bury my face between your thighs and lick you until you scream my name."

Welp, she was struck dumb. That's all there was to it. Here she sat staring at a BBQ sandwich with her brain-juice on E. She wished something intelligent would just surprise-plop out of her mouth, but nope, all she could say was, "Hot. Hot…boy."

"I'd dig my fingers into your legs as I made you come over and over, back all arched on the bed, eyes closed because all you can think about is my tongue sliding inside of you."

She was getting dumber. All she could do now was blink slow.

"And then when you got too sensitive to go another time, I'd push your knees farther apart, crawl over you, slide my dick inside you, and go at you slow until you came again. I'd leave you on that bed, full of my cum, wondering what the fuck I just did to your body."

Mayday.

She was done.

Stick a fork in her.

"I wish I could say something sexy back to you right now, but my whole brain is focused on the mental picture you just put in my head. That was glorious." She cleared her throat. "Well done, dirty boy."

"Mmmm," he said, more growl than anything. "I want to make you a dirty girl. Someday, come back."

"Someday," she murmured.

"Someday soon. I'm here."

Me, too. She was still here, an hour away from him. She dropped her gaze to the receipt taped to the side of her BBQ sandwich wrapper fluttering in the breeze from the vent above her. $10.10. Ha. Remi shook her head and huffed a breath. That number…

She was on a secret mission she couldn't abandon just to be in Kamp's arms again. Not yet. She had to do this first. As each minute passed, there was something telling her this journey was important.

"Hey, Kamp?"

"Yeah?"

"I'm really proud you finished your shift today."

"Yeah, well, Grim turned into the Reaper in the middle of the day and attacked my machine for half an hour, and Rhett worked maybe two hours before he cussed out a mossy log and disappeared into the woods, so you would be the only one who cares that I did a full day's work. We're all going to get fired."

"Do it again tomorrow. Be the leader your Crew needs until Grim can get strong enough."

Kamp snorted. "It don't work like that for us."

"Then make it work."

There were three beats of silence, and then he murmured, "Will you call me when you're safe in the city? Or text me, write a postcard, or send a damn carrier pigeon, anything. I just want to know you get where you're going safe."

Okay, her smile must've been stupidly big because a mother of two sitting a couple tables over looked concerned and was staring at Remi like she was a nut-job. She would be correct.

"You're concerned for my safety, you called just to make sure I was okay after a message from my ex, *and* you said I made you happy for a little while."

"Okay, okaaaay—"

"You really liiiiiike meeee," she sang, "Not just for my bodyyyyy."

"God, I'm hanging up now."

"I'll send you some heart emojis."

"Bye, Novak."

"I'm not hanging up until you call me by my real name—"

The line went dead and Remi pouted. The phone rang immediately, and when she answered, all Kamp said was, "Talk to you soon, Remi." And then it went dead again, but her pouting was through! She texted him a heart emoji and a laughing face just to mess with him, and while she snarfed her sandwich, she giggled at herself for being the most amusing court jester in all the land. Up until the moment he sent her a heart emoji back with no laughing face.

Remi slurped a pickle and stared at that little red symbol of love.

Wait, did he really like her? Like she liked him?

Be cool. Don't respond.

Poop emoji. Send.

Aw crap. She was going to die single.

TEN

Remington had been completely confident in her decision to find Sophia…until now.

Until the moment she was sitting out in front of Daisy Duke's Flower Shop, staring in the window at an intimidatingly beautiful curly-haired goddess with skin the color of milk chocolate, big doe brown eyes, perfect cheekbones, full lips, and the best damn curves she'd ever seen on another woman. She didn't swing that way, but if she did, Remi would totally have a crush on Sophia. The mother of Kamp's child. His ex-lover. *Oh, gross, get a hold of yourself and don't say 'lover.'*

Here she was in a hoodie, ripped skinny jeans, an old pair of mud-crusted hiking boots, and very little makeup, with wild hair she hadn't bothered to curl today. And here she was going to talk to Sophia about her child like this was any of her business.

Remi searched frantically for a 1010 anywhere but found none. Maybe that was a sign to abort mission.

But she couldn't make herself drive away. She'd come three hours in a stolen truck to talk to this human because what she was doing to Kamp was wrong.

And that thought—protecting Kamp and giving him a better life—was what helped Remi turn off the truck and slide out of the cab.

According to the hours posted on the door, the shop was almost closed. Sophia seemed to be the only one inside since Remi could only hear one heartbeat besides her own.

Sophia was working on an arrangement behind the counter when Remi walked in. The bell on the door dinged clearly, and Sophia turned around with a big, bright smile.

Maybe this wasn't Sophia. Maybe Sophia was a very non-intimidating troll with bad manners who owned twenty-seven tarantulas and only drank pickle juice.

"Hi, welcome in! I'm Sophia."

Aw, dangit. "Hello," Remi said, sidling up to the counter. Goodness, how did she even begin? She cleared her throat. That didn't help knock the old brain loose, so she cleared her throat again.

"Are you wanting an arrangement?" Sophia asked, twitching her tight curls off her shoulder. They were blond at the ends. So pretty. Remi was way out of her league. If this was Kamp's type, Remi wasn't worth anything more than a casual fling. Sophia was poise and grace, while Remi...well, Remi was a walking disaster.

"Are you okay?" Why did people keep asking her that?

"I'm here with a strange request."

"Okaaay," Sophia drawled out, looking disturbed.

Remi blew out a steadying breath. "I know Kamp."

Sophia's face went completely blank, and she froze like a garden gnome. A beautiful, beautiful garden gnome.

"And he really wants to be a part of Raider's life," she rushed out, her words tumbling end over end. "I don't have any right to come in here and get involved because I'm sure I only know the surface story of why you keep his son from him. But I see Kamp and how much he hurts missing his cub, and he's not doing very well."

"This is none of your business—"

"I know. Seriously...I know. It's just he doesn't know where you are, or where Raider is, and it isn't fair on him—"

"Fair on him? I watched him attack his own mother. Did he tell you that?"

"Yep. He told me he Turned her."

Sophia frowned. "He did tell you?"

"Well...yeah."

Sophia opened her mouth and shut it again, her frown deepening. "Kamp isn't really a talker. Or a sharer. So I guess you caught me a little off guard. But still, it was awful. I'd never witnessed anything like that, and I was scared for my life. He found out about something I was doing—"

"You mean someone you were doing?"

Anger flashed across her face, and she gritted her teeth. "Judge all you want, but I'm married to the man I fell in love with."

“Okay, but you were still with Kamp. To him, a dominant predator shifter, you were his and he was yours. Nearly any shifter in his position would’ve gone in a rage.”

“Yeah, and when his mother showed up? She was Turned. It was awful. I thought he’d killed her. I don’t want my son around that.”

Around that? Kamp wasn’t a *that*. “*He* is your son’s father.”

“Raider has a father. His name is Todd.”

“No, Sophia. You are a smart and strong woman, and I can tell you know right from wrong. Todd is Raider’s step-father. Raider is a lion cub. Kamp is his dad, and you’re keeping them apart.”

“Yes, and that lion inside of him is a monster. That’s what Todd and I get to deal with. That’s what Kamp did. He put a lion in his mother, put a lion in his son, and I don’t want anything to do with him or his people.”

“But you chose a shifter.”

“My life, my choice.”

“Agreed,” Remi said, nodding. “I completely agree. But the more support Raider has as he grows up, the better. You cutting him off from his dad? That will hurt him so much more than you can even fathom over his lifetime."

Sophia lifted her chin high, and her eyes were rimming with moisture. "He has Todd. It's enough."

"It's not enough. I can see it in your eyes. Raider is having trouble with that lion cub, and he has no adult male lion to teach his animal manners or how to be a lion. You didn't get a deadbeat father for your child, Sophia. I've looked Kamp in the face when he talks about his son. He wants to be present. I mean, hell, he's paying into that child support account with no rights and no hope he'll ever see his boy. He just wants to be a part of his life in any way he can. You're cutting him out of Raider's young years. How many firsts has he missed because of your choice to hide him?"

Sophia shook her head, over and over, and wouldn't meet Remi's eyes anymore. Outside, a car door shut, and when Remi turned around, a little boy was running up to the door. A dark-haired man followed him, but Remi couldn't keep her attention from the boy. He was tall for a four-year-old, lanky, but that would change when he hit maturity. He would likely be every bit as big as Kamp. His skin was lighter than his mothers, and his hair was curly and a sandy-brown tone. One of his eyes was bright green and one was gold. He was holding an old threadbare teddy bear against his chest as he tugged at the heavy door.

After he wiggled in through the space he'd made, he paused when he saw Remi, and a little snarl rattled his throat. Remi was stunned by the boy. Not because of the way he looked, but by the sheer power of the little lion he had tucked inside of him. Brawler, indeed, with an angelic face. He was the perfect combination of Kamp and his mother.

"You should go now," Sophia said to her sternly as Raider made his way around the counter to his mom.

"Please just think about what I've said."

"Think about what?" the man asked as he came through the door. He smelled like fur, and his eyes were too bright blue to pass for human. Todd.

"This woman knows Kamp," Sophia told him. "He's found us."

"No, he hasn't," Remi said, easing back from the hyena shifter. The last thing she needed was her bear to go into defense mode right now. "He doesn't even know I'm here. He is in a last chance Crew because his animal can't handle the loss of his cub."

"A last chance Crew?" Sophia murmured. She lifted Raider into her arms. "I'm just trying to make the best decision for my boy."

"Are you?"

"He Turned his mother."

"That's the nature of shifters. We aren't perfect. Our mistakes are on a high-stakes scale, but you can't punish him for being half-animal. You can't punish him for his instincts. Not like this."

"We have all we need," she said, lifting her chin. But there was a shake in her voice that said she didn't believe her own words.

"You need a bigger team, and you know it. One you can trust. One who will do anything to keep him pointed in the right direction, right along with you guys. I'm from a place where there was a big team in raising cubs. I don't know what I would've done without that support." Remi moved to the counter slowly, peripheral on the hyena shifter. She scratched Kamp's address onto a notepad, along with her phone number and his. "Please just consider letting him be part of your lives. For you guys, but also for Kamp."

"I know Kamp," Raider said softly. "That's my lion

dad."

Remi smiled and nodded. "Clever boy." She handed Sophia the paper. "That's my number. Kamp's is the one at the bottom. I don't know, maybe you already have it, but just in case you ever need anything. I won't tell him I was here. Your family decisions are up to you, but you should know he would give anything to be a part of this." Remi gave Raider one last smile and committed his cute little face to memory just in case this was the only time she ever saw him. "He feels big."

"What do you mean?" Todd asked in a gravelly voice.

"I don't know… He just feels special." It was an instinct in her gut that told her Raider would have a big story someday.

She made her way to the door, but just before she left, Todd asked, "You said you don't know what you would've done without a big support system. What are you?"

Remi didn't usually tell shifters who she was because they had expectations through rumors of her father. But something compelled her to own who she was with these people.

"I'm a Novak Grizzly."

And just as she let the door swing closed behind her, she heard Todd whisper, "Holy shit."

ELEVEN

Exhausted, Remi sat down on the bed at the Marriot in Eugene. She was drained and didn't feel like driving the three hours back. Really, she just needed to sit for a minute and absorb everything that had happened and plot her next move. Or stay here for a couple of days perhaps. She was definitely already fired from her barista job in the city, so why not spend some savings while she tried to figure her life out?

She plopped back on the mattress, legs and arms spread out like she was a star. She missed him—Kamp.

She dialed his number.

"Hey, you just made my night with this call," he

said, sounding so happy to talk to her.

She couldn't help but smile up at the ceiling fan. "What are you up to?"

"Waiting for a call from a pretty girl to tell me she is safe."

"I'm a grizzly shifter. I'm always safe," she muttered.

His chuckle warmed her blood, and she began to relax. "I'm safe where I'm going. Now for real, paint me a picture. What are you doing right now?"

"Uh, right now, I'm sitting under the awning, taking a break from working on this four-wheeler to talk to you."

"Son of a biscuit-eater!"

Remi frowned. "Was that Rhett?"

"Yep. I'm also listening to him curse everything in existence because I made him work on the other four-wheeler. He just smashed his finger."

"You made him work? How?" She couldn't imagine Rhett doing anything he was told.

"I threatened to start a rumor in town that he has scabies if he doesn't do it."

"Hmm. Nicely done."

"I hate both of you," Rhett assured them. "And

furthermore, where is my truck?" he yelled.

"So, how's your day?" Kamp asked, ignoring Rhett's tantrum.

"It's going...okay. Not phenomenal, but not horrible."

"Sounds like a good enough day in my book."

Rhett called out over the phone, "I wish you would've taken Kamp with you when you left. He's a life-ruiner. Better your life be ruined than mine."

"Fix up the four-wheeler good!" Remi sang.

She was pretty sure she heard Rhett mutter the word "hate" to himself.

"I'm about to send a picture through," Kamp said. "Are you ready?"

"I'm super-ready." When her phone vibrated, she looked at the image that came through. It was of a waterfall and the river below it.

"Oh, that's beautiful! Where is that?"

"It's maybe a quarter mile hike from the trailer park. It's called Whiskey Pick Falls."

Rhett stopped his hate-song long enough to yell, "He means Whiskey Dick Falls."

Kamp's sigh tapered off into a growl. "The sign says Whiskey Pick, but I'm pretty sure Rhett has ruined the name forever."

Remi laughed and admitted, "I like Whiskey Dick Falls just fine."

"Also," Kamp said, "I have a couple of beers in the fridge with our names on them."

"What do you mean?"

"Me and you—we'll shotgun them someday. And there's plenty of trees to climb here, too."

And then it hit her. He was offering up the things she'd told him she'd missed about Damon's Mountains. Shot-gunning a beer, riding four-wheelers, climbing trees, jumping off Bear Trap Falls, and...

"You already Changed with a whole Crew," he murmured. "Sure, we were all clawing each other up, but you were born a Gray Back. Pretty sure that was just another Tuesday for you."

"You listened to me."

"Huh? What? I can't hear you. I wasn't listening."

She giggled. "No, I'm serious. You really listened. That means a lot. Kamp?"

"Yeah?"

"If I told you I like tulips, would you remember?"

"Of course. I remember everything you say."

There was such honesty in every word, she believed him completely.

"Barf. Gaaaag. Gag and barf. Garf." Well, Rhett was being his normal, charming, moment-ruining self.

"Will you ever come back?" Kamp asked.

Remi sighed and admitted softly, "I don't know what I'm doing."

There was a beat of silence, and then he told her, "That's okay. You're doing just fine, Remi. No one knows what they're doing, not really. Anyone who seems to have it all together is just good at pretending. Someday, if you get tired of the city again, the four-wheelers will be all gassed up and ready for you."

Right now, in this moment, she wished she could hug him. Wished he could wrap her up tight in his strong arms and make her feel safe. Wished she could end the day with a homecooked meal and then blasting through his mountains on an ATV instead of staring at a room service menu on a cold bedside table.

For the first time in a long time, she felt homesick.

And for the first time ever, homesickness wasn't for a place.

It was for a person.

TWELVE

Remi sounded a little sad, and there was this bottomless instinct to make her feel better. Kamp didn't know why and was helpless to explain it. All he knew was this trailer park felt completely hollow without her.

How could a person have such an impact on a place in such a short amount of time?

He couldn't stop thinking about her. How her skin felt under his fingertips, the little helpless noises she uttered when he'd made her feel good, her freckles and soft hair, her eyes that had animated to match every word she spoke. The way she could look right through a man to his soul and not run away. How brave she was when she'd gone after him. How fearless her bear was. How loyal her little heart seemed to be to that ratty old trailer at the end of the park. How funny she was. How independent. How she balanced confidence and insecurity in a completely endearing way that made him want to take care of her and watch her be a badass all at once. How she could dress down and hang with the boys but, oh, he knew she could clean herself up and be a bombshell. This girl had layers, and he was hungry to learn more. He was starving to learn everything about her.

She was the most interesting person he'd ever met, and now this city shifter had all of his attention. He didn't want to beg because it had to be her decision to come back but, fuck, he would sell his bones to have her here, just for a chance at...something.

She took the edge off everything, and he was addicted to the happy feeling and relief that washed through him when she was around.

Remington Novak was the most beautiful distraction he'd ever known.

And she was gone.

Everyone always left.

"Honey, I'm hoooome," Rhett sang out as he

crawled up the firewood processing machine.

"Fuck. Off," Kamp called over the blaring country music.

"I come bearing gifts. Get it? Bear-ing gifts?"

"I have two hours before I'm quitting. If you have time to make up riddles, you have time to finish the shift with me."

"Ew. No. Look, I made you a picture." Rhett slapped it against the outside of Kamp's window. It was a horribly drawn lion fucking a teddy bear.

"You're sick, dude."

"It's the first picture of you two! Do you want me to hang it on your fridge?" Rhett waited with a big dumb grin on his face. "Yes?" He nodded. "Okay, I'll put it on your fridge."

"Stay out of my house!"

"Your house is my house!" Rhett called over his shoulder as he walked away.

"You're saying it wrong. And don't drink my beer!"

The asshole threw a middle finger over his shoulder and, for a moment, Kamp gave serious thought to chopping down the tree right next to Rhett and squishing him out of existence. So tempting.

First picture of them. A deep ache spread through his chest, and he cut the engine and hunched over the pain. He scrubbed his hands down his face. His body hurt. Three fights since Remi had left, and for what? They didn't make him feel better. Not anymore. They didn't steady him out like they used to. Fighting Grim just made him glitch and feel as if he needed to keep fighting, and fighting, and fighting until he didn't feel anything anymore.

Pissed off at the world, he muttered a curse and shook his head. He hadn't wanted something in so long. He hadn't dared to crave attention from anyone, because look what happened? He would still be alone in the end.

Movement caught his attention at the edge of the tree line he was working. Grim stood there, battered to hell, claw marks all over his torso and arms, eyes bright gold, black Mohawk a mess. He twitched his chin for Kamp to get out of the processor.

Addict. That's what the Reaper was. Fighting fed his demon. Last chance Crew, and the Alpha was the sickest of them all.

With a sigh, Kamp shoved the door open and hopped out, his boots squishing into the mud.

"Again?" he asked.

"Always," Grim rumbled in a deep, snarling voice.

"Why?"

"You don't want the fight?" Grim asked, an empty, knowing smile spreading across his face. "I'm helping you out, Kamp."

"By bleeding me?"

A long snarl rattled his throat, and he took two steps closer. "By letting you bleed me."

"Maybe I should just kill you and take the Crew."

Grim lifted his chin and looked down his nose at Kamp, eyes nothing but gold slits. "You think you and Rhett would be better off? You think you could run these mountains better?"

"Probably a pinecone could run this Crew better."

"Then end it."

Kamp frowned. "What?"

Grim's nostrils flared as he inhaled. "End it already." There was an order to his tone, one that urged Kamp's instincts to obey. "Do it."

Kamp shook his head and backed up. "Stop it, Grim."

"Do it," Grim said again, stalking forward. "Put me out of my misery. Fight to the death. You know you want it."

Yes, his lion whispered. *We want that.*

"Grim, I said stop it! I'm not throwing an Alpha Challenge. We aren't doing this. No one is going to die."

"Yet."

Kill him.

Kamp slapped the side of his head and shook it as hard as he could to get his animal to shut up.

Kill him and take the Crew. He wants you to.

"Stop fucking with my head," Kamp said to Grim through gritted teeth. "What's wrong with you?"

"Nothing," Grim answered, his eyes flashing as bright as the sun. "And everything."

"I'm so sick of riddles, Grim. I've had a couple of bad days, and I just want to finish my shift and get on to my next day. Eat, work, sleep, eat, work, sleep until I go crazy enough with the monotony of my life to actually give in to an Alpha Challenge. I got nothing but that machine, Grim." Kamp jammed a finger at the processor. "Metal. That's all I got, and I swear if you and Rhett get us fired off this mountain, I'll make sure you live forever. I'll walk right behind you through your entire life and protect you from any harm that comes your way. I'll pledge my fealty to your survival just to piss you off. You want to die? Ask Rhett to do it."

"Rhett can't get the job done."

"Then too fuckin' bad! Guess you'll just have to put in some effort and run this Crew."

"You have a voice in your head, don't you?" Grim yelled, his voice echoing through the mountains. "One voice. One lion dictating when you fight, fuck, sleep, eat…one voice telling you what to do."

Kamp didn't know how to respond. The woods around them had gone eerily quiet.

Grim leaned down, picked up a fallen branch, and chucked that thing like a javelin with such power it sank into a massive tree and hovered there, six feet above the ground, vibrating against the split trunk.

Kamp had never seen strength like that. Grim had been hiding what he was capable of, and now Kamp really was treading dangerous territory.

Chest heaving, Grim gave Kamp his back. He hooked his hands on his hips and dropped his head. "I have two," he uttered in a hoarse voice. And then he walked away.

"Wait, what? Two what?" Kamp asked, following a

few steps. "Two voices? You got two voices in you? Grim, hold up!" He walked faster, then jogged after him. "You got two lions inside of you?"

Grim cut to the right suddenly and disappeared behind a huge tree trunk. Kamp pushed his legs harder and skidded on the pine needles that blanketed the forest floor when he reached the stump, but on the other side, there was no one there. He searched in vain. The Alpha had disappeared like he'd never existed in these woods at all.

Two lions? Was that what Grim really meant? He was two animals? Holy shit. Kamp was slowly going insane, and he only had one lion running his life. He couldn't even imagine being the vessel for two predator animals.

****

Remi had heard it all.

She stood there between two pines, staring across the clearing at Kamp as he searched for Grim. Two lions in him. That's what the Alpha had meant…right? How awful.

But what was even more gut-wrenching was Kamp's face. He scanned the woods with a deep frown, face pale as if all the blood had drained from it.

He looked like he was going to be sick.

Slowly, she stepped out of the woods. Kamp's green and gold gaze jerked right to her. He froze there like a pond in the middle of a cold winter. The brush crackled under her sneakers as she made her way past the logging machine and the stack of firewood he'd been cutting with those big blades. She came to a stop a few feet away from him.

"Tell me you're real," he murmured. "Tell me you're really here."

"I'm here. And I'm real. Here…feel…" She made her way to him and slid her arms around his waist.

Dropping his hands from his hips, Kamp sighed, expelling tension from his rigid body as he did. Oh, he'd told her he didn't like touch, so she wasn't hurt he didn't hug her back at first. That sigh of relief counted for more. And when he rested his whiskered chin on top of her head and slid his arms around her shoulders, she melted against him. This right here was the best feeling in the world. It was like the first breath after she'd been drowning.

A hundred times over the last couple of days, she'd wondered why he had such an effect on her. A hundred times, she'd tried to talk herself out of liking him. A hundred times she'd tried to convince herself she was just crazy, or broken after the break-up, or that her heart was just trying to latch on to the first man who showed her kindness...but as she stood in the shadow of the pines, in the strength of Kamp's arms, her heart soaring because it felt at home, none of those insecurities mattered. All that mattered was that Kamp made sense to her.

"I'll have to put Grim down someday soon," he murmured. And, oh, his voice held the grit of sadness. "I hate him for doing this."

"For doing what?"

His heart beat from his chest against her cheek so steadily. Ten beats before he murmured, "He just made me care about this Crew."

A slow smile stretched across Remi's face, and she leaned back so she could see his eyes after he admitted his heart had been thawed.

"It's your fault, too, you know," he said, brushing his fingertips along her cheek. "You came in here and brought me back to life, and now I have work to do."

"What work? Becoming Alpha?"

Kamp shook his head slowly, eyes never leaving hers. "No. That's not my fate, Novak. Nothing in me wants that title. Not when it means taking Grim out to get it. I mean, now I actually have to put in effort here, try to prop up a bad king."

"Mmmm," she murmured, running her fingernails gently up and down his back. "Where I'm from, there are no bad kings. Only damaged ones. And the Crew who props them up are just as important as the Alphas."

Kamp huffed a breath. "Only a Gray Back would find out an Alpha has two lions and call him salvageable."

"I'm built for this," she whispered through a grin.

"Built for what?" Was that hope in his eyes?

"I'm built for a C-Team Crew like this one."

The corners of his lips lifted just slightly. "Tell me again that you're real."

Remi pushed up on her tiptoes and pressed her lips to his. She loved how he tasted, how soft he went against her. He was very tough, very hard, very closed off...with most. With her, he was different. She had no idea how long they stayed like that—kissing like they had all the time in the world. All she knew was that right here with him, everything felt like it would be okay. Maybe this was what falling in love was supposed to be like. Perhaps she'd just gotten it wrong in the first place so she could have this epiphany moment. *Ah, this is what it's supposed to feel like.* Maybe she'd gotten it wrong in the first place so she could fully appreciate Kamp. So her bear could know exactly who it was she wanted.

Kamp's hand rested gently on the back of her neck, and he pushed her backward, his other hand steady on the small of her back as he laid her down. His lips massaged her as he kissed her. God, his weight on top of her felt so good, like a comfort blanket that made her feel all safe and warm. With each layer of clothing he removed from her, his fingers dug into her skin perfectly—breasts, hips, the back of her knee as he bent her leg and lifted it to encase him between her thighs. His lips left hers to trail down her jaw line, to suck on her earlobe, bite her neck gently, and then he pulled her nipple into his mouth and sucked it until she was moaning, gripping the back of his hair. Remi's body moved against him like waves crashing onto a beach.

Down, down he went, trailing kisses and fire until he reached the space between her thighs. His eyes were bright gold and green when he looked back up at her, and they sparked with wickedness. His smile was perfectly feral.

He ran his tongue up her slit, and when she gasped and rolled her hips toward him, he murmured, "Beg me."

She hadn't done this before! No man's mouth had ever touched her there, but right as her insecurities reared up, Kamp ran his tongue up her folds again and struck her dumb. Over and over, he licked, slow and controlled, the tip of his tongue hitting her clit. Her legs trembled with want. She needed more, so she did something else for the first time ever. She begged.

"Please Kamp, I need you. I want to feel you in me."

"Good girl," he purred, and then his tongue slid deep inside her.

With a moan of ecstasy, she slid her fingers into his hair and let herself get lost in the stroking of his tongue. His head bobbed between her legs, and his arms were wrapped around her thighs, holding her tight against his face, as though he never wanted to stop tasting her. The purr that emanated from his throat rattled against her sensitive nub, and nothing had *ever* felt like this. So sexy. So perfect.

The purring sensation between her legs vibrated stronger, until she rode the edge of climax. It felt better every time his tongue pushed into her. Purring, purring...growling. Growling?

Felt too good to pay much attention. Almost there...

The growling got louder, and Kamp jerked back suddenly. He crawled over her and unfastened his jeans in a rush. And before the shock of his blurred movement even wore off, Kamp slid his thick, hard dick into her. He buried himself deep. Hard and fast, he slammed into her, his powerful body tense, his face contorted and his canine teeth longer and sharper as he bared them. He gripped the back of her hair and, oh dear lord, this was the hottest thing she'd ever been a part of. The intensity in his eyes alone was enough to make her come, but when he threw his head back and yelled a feral sound, his cock throbbing inside of her, she lost it. She cried out as her body pulsed to match his, her release so potent she couldn't think a single thought. She could only watch his powerful body as he came inside of her. He jerked and twitched, dragging out every throbbing sensation, his stomach clenching every time he released more seed inside her. He was absolutely captivating when he came.

"I almost bit you," he ground out, locking his arms on either side of her head.

"W-what?"

"I almost claimed you, right there on your thigh. It's all I was thinking about while I was eating you out." Kamp's lip snarled up. "You should know the monster you're bedding."

When he eased his dick from her, warmth spilled down her leg. Eyes downcast, he leaned down and kissed her throat and lips before he stood. "I'm sorry," he murmured as he strode away, buckling up his jeans.

Remi was at a total loss. Sorry for what? The urge to claim her? She'd dreamed of a claiming mark like human girls dreamed of wedding days.

Remi sat up, anger pulsing through her body that he was running from her.

Through the woods, her voice echoed as she called out, "I'm still real, and I'm still here!"

Kamp skidded to a stop. "Fuck!" rang out. He scrubbed his hands through his hair. "Woman, did you not just hear me? I told you I almost just fucking claimed you. Claimed you! Look around here." Kamp waved his hand at the felled logs and the processor. "It should be your choice to tether yourself to this life. Not my animal's."

Carefully she asked, "Is it only your animal choosing me? Is that the problem?"

Kamp huffed a breath and stared off to the side, his head shaking slightly. "I don't know how to do this."

"What? Giving me the best bone of my life and then running away? Scaredy cat," she accused him.

"Don't call me that."

"Scaredy lion," she corrected herself, standing. "You wanted me to come back, but you didn't want to actually get close to me. Right? Getting close to people is scary?"

He nodded. "Getting close to you. To Grim. To Rhett. You'll all leave."

"Or we won't. But you'll never know if you keep everyone at arm's length." She stomped toward him, good and pissed, and then blasted him in the shoulder with hers as she passed. "I don't like feeling unimportant."

Kamp put his arms around her from behind and forced her to stand still. She growled, "Careful, Cat, I apparently don't like feeling trapped either."

"You aren't trapping me. Fuck…just wait…just hold still…I need a second. My head is so loud."

"Was it the first time you ever felt like claiming a girl?" she whispered.

"Woman, I just asked for a few seconds of quiet."

"You asked the wrong girl for that. I don't mind rules well."

There was a loaded second in the silent woods, and then he snorted and dropped his head against the back of hers. He let off an explosive sigh. "If I mark you too soon, you won't choose to stay here on your own. I'm a mess, Remi. You're a mess, and everyone here is a mess, and I don't want to fuck this all up. I always do that, and I want you to stick. I want you to pick me in some quiet moment when you are thinking clear. In some proud moment when I do something that makes you know I'm the one, and you smile at me and tell me to do it. Claim you. And if you never get there, that's okay. But I want you to know the kind of man I am, and tricking you into staying here with me too soon isn't how I want to win your heart. I want you to give it to me free and clear someday."

Remi's lip trembled, and her eyes burned as she focused on the bark of the tree in front of her.

Smart man.

She slid her hands to his forearms that were wrapped around her and squeezed a silent *It's okay*. He'd made her place here completely up to her. She couldn't be angry with him for that. She admired the patient hunter inside of him. He was giving her room to breathe, test this life, and see if it's what she really wanted.

"When is your shift over?" she asked.

He swallowed hard and murmured against her ear, "An hour and a half." So he had plans to finish his shift. To finish what he started.

Good man.

She drew his scarred knuckles to her lips and pressed a kiss onto them. And then she told him, "I'll see you then."

She offered him a quick smile as she walked away to gather up her clothes, so he wouldn't see how choked up she was over his thoughtfulness. Over him taking care of her heart in the only way he knew how.

"You sure are a beautiful sight, Remi Novak," he called as she left, her clothes clutched tight in her hand. "I would've come to the city to find you if you didn't come back here. You should know that."

Brave man.

There were the butterflies, her companions as she hiked back toward the trailer park. The engine noise of the processor was her soundtrack. And a few minutes later, she found herself staring at the side of 1010 with her mouth hanging open wide enough to catch flies.

The hole was gone.

It had been patched with plywood and painted to match the rest of the trailer.

He'd fixed it for her, even knowing she might never come back.

He'd.

Fixed.

It.

But as she stood there in the waning light of a cool autumn evening, staring at the *thing* that Kamp had pieced back together, she didn't know whether the *thing* she thought of was 1010...or her heart.

She would do as he asked and be patient for a

claiming mark, but down to her bones she already knew—she was his and he was hers.

Smart, good, brave man.

Her man.

THIRTEEN

Rhett had been hiding a little secret.

A little mountain-sized secret.

He was a thief and a hoarder, apparently, because Remi was staring at a pile of letters in the bottom drawer of the dresser in 1010 where Rhett used to live. And most of those letters were addressed to Grim and Kamp. About half of the letters had red bold words across the front: *Open Immediately, Final Notice*, and *Do Not Discard.*

What the hell?

Being the nosey little monster-bear she was, Remi scooped up an armful and tossed them on the bed, and then she picked one out of the pile and ripped into it.

This one was for Grim. It was a spreadsheet of the numbers they were supposed to hit for logging. It was broken down by types of logs, planks, and bundles of firewood. There was a column of the numbers they'd apparently hit for the month of August, and then a column of totals of how much they had missed their quotas by. It was a ridiculous amount.

"Geez," she murmured, reaching for another one. This one was for the month of July. There was a letter from an unnamed person who apparently owned these mountains, lighting up Grim for failing so epically. The next was how much their wages were being garnished. The next was a threat to fire all three of them. The next two were voided paychecks. The next was a bill for a new machine. The next...was addressed to Kamp, but the handwriting was a chicken scratch she would know anywhere.

"Dad?" This was one letter she couldn't bring herself to open. It wasn't for her. The others, okay. She was hatching a plan to get this Crew up and running, and she needed to know how bad off they were. But a personal letter to the man she was falling for? From the man who'd raised her?

Opening it would be stealing.

Shaken, she folded it in half and shoved it in her back pocket, reached for her favorite, worn flannel shirt, pulled it over her black tank top, and made her way outside to wait for Kamp. He would be home any minute now.

Restless, she didn't settle on the porch stairs to watch the sunset like she'd intended to. Instead, she made her way to the back of the trailer park.

Rhett sat outside in an old green lawn chair leaned up against the shed while he plucked the strings of a guitar. "Here for some of the stash? Sorry, Princess Novak. The Penis Juice is off limits to outsiders."

"Don't you have work to do?"

"Don't have to work. I'm a rich, entitled asshole who can live out my days on the money I have in savings."

"Are you serious?"

"No. I sell Kamp's beer on the side and pocket the money."

"Again...are you fucking serious?"

"Maybe not but probably so."

"You're a terrible person."

Rhett rolled his eyes and sighed an annoyed sound. "I shove his part of the profits in a sock under his mattress. I keep waiting for him to find it, but he never reaches for the Glock he has hidden under there." He switched easily to another song that sounded familiar. "After a month, the money stash was getting pretty decent, so now it's fun to see how big I can grow it before he figures it out."

Huh.

"Where do you sell it?" she asked, taking a seat next to Rhett's chair.

"In town around the bars. Portland and the billion little towns outside of it. Bars everywhere here. Lots of bikers drinking Pen15 Juice."

Remi laughed. "You mean Penis Juice."

"Yep. Speaking of which, I'm taking my truck back. You killed my business for a couple days. I'm supposed to be making deliveries."

"Your business is in these mountains with your Crew, Rhett. I found your hidden stash of mail."

She thought he would at least look guilty over being busted, but he shrugged his shoulders and started strumming the guitar again. He was actually really good. And then she figured out from where she recognized those guitar riffs. He was playing an intro to Beck Brothers song. She wondered if he was any good at singing.

"Why do you hide the mail?"

"Because it keeps the stress off Grim. And less stress means we survive the Reaper."

"You could keep stress off him by actually working, by hitting your quotas, and then you won't get that mail anymore and you can all keep your jobs."

"Piss off, Novak. You don't know how it is around here."

His anger stung. "I'm trying to figure it out."

"Well, stop trying," he gritted out, standing. "Just stop. We all hate each other. You get that much, right? We *hate* each other. We didn't choose this Crew, none of us did. We got thrown together because we don't have anywhere else to go. We aren't some epic friendship waiting to happen."

"But you do little things to take care of Kamp and Grim. I see it. Little things to protect them. You keep them from killing each other, you take claw marks to your ribs to take their attention off each other during fights. You hide letters and stock money away for

Kamp, and for what? Why, Rhett? I'll tell you why. It's because deep down you do care about them."

"Fuck this," he muttered, sauntering off. "I don't care about anyone. Not you, not Kamp, and definitely not you!" he yelled, ramming his finger at Grim, who was sitting against a tree not more than fifteen yards away as if he'd been there the whole time. Creepy. "I don't give a single shit about anyone or anything, so you trying to find reasons for my actions?" He turned and walked backward, his smile cruel. "You can't determine the intentions of someone whose lost their mind, Novak."

"Why did you slash my tires?" she asked, standing up.

"Because I like destruction."

"But I heard you when I drove away. You said you wanted me to stay. Why?"

Rhett huffed a breath, gave her the finger, and then gave one to Grim while he was at it. Kamp came out of the woods, a frown marring his face.

"Why?" she asked again, louder.

Rhett meandered right past Kamp, gripping the neck of his guitar in a stranglehold. He didn't answer, nor did he turn around.

"You shouldn't dig up graves here," Grim said in a raspy voice.

"Fuck off, Grim," Kamp growled. "Don't tell her what she can and can't do. You ain't her Alpha."

Grim turned an empty smile on Kamp. "But wouldn't that be something? Being the Alpha of a Novak Grizzly. She would be like a trophy for the Crew." But there was something strange in Grim's tone, as though he didn't really believe in what he was saying.

"She isn't a trophy, asshole," Kamp said, stepping between Grim and Remi. "She's the best of us."

"Us? There is no *us*, Kamp. There's you, Rhett, and me...and her." He turned his lightened gold gaze on her. "You're messing with the balance around here."

Remi narrowed her eyes at him. "You gonna tell me to leave? I would eat you, Grim. And you forgot one. It's Kamp and Rhett, you and the Reaper, and me. You want to be on the mountain all alone with the Reaper? Go ahead and chase us off then."

Stupid boys. She was messing with the balance? She was trying to help! She pulled open the door to the shed and slammed it closed behind her. Only the door wasn't super sturdy, and it cracked, right down the middle. Half of it fell off with a dusty crash, so now she had to see Grim's dumb, smiling face outside.

And something about that just proved to be the last straw. Her bear was pissed, she was pissed, and everything was tinted in red. And, yeah…she sometimes had a temper problem and, yeah, she was about to throw a full-fledged fit, but damn it all, Rhett and Grim had it comin'.

"Rhett!" she bellowed as she kicked open the broken door. "Rhett! Rhett!" Remi clenched her hands at her side and got real determined to annoy him into paying attention. Tossing her chin back, she roared his name at the sky. "Rheeeeeett! Rheee—"

"What, what, what, WHAT?" he yelled, crashing through the brush like a pissed-off bull elephant.

"Crew meeting! Shit's a-changin' around here!" she screamed at the top of her lungs. "I was gonna try to be gentle about this and patient and take my time getting to know the ins and outs of this Crew before I started encouraging you to make positive changes in your lives, but fuck that! Seven a.m. tomorrow, all of you start work."

All three men stared at her with eyes round as dinner plates, as though she'd lost every last bit of her mind.

"Oh, she gets a country accent when she's pissed," Rhett said quietly.

"Seven a.m., I'll be waiting out front of the trailer park, and if you three aren't out of bed and headed to your machines, I'm going to do horrible things to wake you up."

"Like what?" Grim asked, his frown so deep it furrowed his forehead.

"Dude," Kamp muttered. "She's on a tirade. Stop interrupting."

"Like Change in your trailer and rip everything to shreds, including you."

"Wait, what if it's Kamp whose late?" Rhett asked.

"What?" she yelled.

"If you maim Kamp, he can't stick his pickle in your lady cavern."

Kamp slapped Rhett upside his head. "What the fuck, man?"

"I'm saying it's not really fair for you to get free passes!" Rhett said, rubbing his hair back into place.

"I'm the only one who's finished a whole shift since we moved out here to BFE, you prick!"

"I finished one, one time," Rhett argued, arching

his eyebrows.

"When?" Grim asked.

"When you weren't paying attention." Rhett looked smug as a beetle on a turd right now.

She might actually kill all of them and just put everyone out of their misery.

"Anyways," she punched out, "you'll work like you're supposed to, you'll hit your numbers, you'll get whoever runs these mountains off your back, and you'll feed the lumber yard. And once a week, we are going to barbecue."

"I don't like barbecue," Rhett muttered.

Glaring at Rhett, Grim growled, "I swear to God I'm gonna kill you."

Kamp sighed and called Rhett out, "Everyone likes barbecue, and you spend every Tuesday night at Hopper's eating brisket sandwiches, so cut it out with your bullshit."

"Okay, stalker, I go to Hoppers because there's booze and hot girls with perky tits there. I eat the sandwich because it's half off on Tuesdays so it would be a sin to ignore such a good deal on meat."

Remi was actually breaking out in rage-hives. Was that a thing? She scratched at the raised itchy bumps on her face. Her bear wanted to turn Rhett and Grim into poop about now.

She counted to three in her head so she wouldn't scream. "Work and bond. That's the point," she said. "This Crew sucks balls right now, and I deserve better. So do the three of you."

The boys all went still as their attention froze on her. "What do you mean you deserve better?" Grim asked suspiciously.

She looked the Alpha dead in the eyes and clenched her fists at her sides as her stubborn streak grew as wide as the Grand Canyon. "I'm not going anywhere. And this," she said, twirling her finger at the three of them. "This doesn't work for anyone. You've been doin' it wrong, boys. Time to shape up."

"We're not listening to some hyped-up woman trying to change everything around here," Grim snarled. "I think it's time for you to leave."

"Or *you* can leave," she retorted. "As it stands, no one would miss you."

Grim snarled a terrifying sound. "Listen here, you—"

"No *you* listen! You're fine with staying stagnant, but that's your problem. You aren't growing. You're staying exactly the same, and has that worked for you? Huh?" She turned to Rhett. "What was your last Crew?"

After a few seconds, Rhett answered, "Saga Pride."

Kamp tensed up. "Wait, isn't your last name Saga?"

For the first time since she'd met him, Remi witnessed Rhett completely close down. He crossed his arms over his chest, and his eyes went dead.

Realizing he would get no more from Rhett about his old pride, Kamp answered low, "No Crew for me. I was raised around humans. This Crew is my first."

When Remi looked at Grim, his smile turned downright unsettling. "Tarian Pride."

"Holy shit, are you serious?" When Rhett took a couple steps back from him, Remi totally understood the instinct. The Tarian Pride were monsters.

"High ranking?" Remi asked with her face all scrunched up. *Please say no.*

"Yep."

"Aw man, we're so screwed," Rhett muttered.

Kamp was standing right next to her and looked down at Remi. Trouble swirled in his mismatched eyes. "It's a problem that none of us even knew these simple answers about each other before now. We've been here for months and didn't even know our old Prides and Crews? Remi's right. We need a change. It would be nice to not be the only one finishing shifts. It would be nice to have some trust in you guys to help me get stuff done."

"Veto. That sounds boring." Rhett gave the peace sign and walked away.

Grim turned and made a beeline for the woods. "I'm gonna go kill stuff," he snarled and then disappeared behind a tree. "Fight you soon, Kamp," his voice echoed back to them. Oh, fantastic.

"We need a Crew name!" Remi called.

"The Never Gonna Happens," Rhett answered without turning around.

"Well," Kamp said, draping his arm around her shoulders. "The first Crew meeting went well."

"Went well? We got nothing accomplished."

"Grim didn't kill anyone and neither did you."

"Well, there's that," she grumbled, glaring at where the other two men had disappeared.

"Bright side, you get to raise hell on 'em in the morning when they don't wake up. After giving me a blow job, of course."

Remi smacked his stony abs, but it only stung her knuckles. He didn't even flinch. Annoying right now. But also sexy. And then it was annoying that it was sexy.

Kamp chuckled and pulled her tight against his side. "You look hot when you're pouting."

"I'm not pouting. I'm internally raging."

Kamp picked her up in a rush and wrapped her legs around him, then spun her in a circle so fast it left her breathless. All she could do was hold onto the back of his neck as her stomach dipped like she was on a roller coaster. When he slowed, his lips crashed onto hers, and she could taste his smile. Easing away, he said, "I was going to take you skinny dipping at Whiskey Dick Falls, but now I have to fix the door you judo chopped. I don't want a mouse getting in."

"Well, where I'm from, having a mouse is lucky. Big old gnarly balls on him is preferable."

Kamp snorted. "Okay, that's weird. In that case, we need to go to the pet store and buy them out. You picked damn-near the unluckiest Crew in the known universe." He kissed her once more and settled her on her feet. "I'm gonna go get my tools. Don't wreck anything while I'm gone." He turned with a smirk and then demolished her lady bits with a hotboy wink as he said, "Remi."

Oh, the sound of her name on his lips. She wrapped her arms around the butterflies threatening to break her middle apart.

All it took was for one person to believe in something. In a Crew. In positive change. In redemption. That was something she'd learned in her years with the Gray Backs. She would be that person until this Crew could believe in themselves. Until they could stand on their own, she would do the standing for them. Kamp deserved stability.

He said his Crew was unlucky, but he didn't see what she did.

This Crew had potential, and she wasn't going to let them quit on each other.

They could do better if only someone had faith in them—and that someone was her.

FOURTEEN

You're super fired.

Remi growled at the text message from her boss at the coffee shop. She'd okayed her to be off for a week but then apparently changed her mind.

"Okay," she said, turning the key on the four-wheeler. "Everything is fine. If the job, my one source of income, the thing that pays all my bills, is gone, then it wasn't meant to be my job."

When she puffed air out of her cheeks, the breath in front of her froze in the frosty morning air. Cold weather would hit these mountains soon.

A wave of excitement took her. Should she be feeling excited that she just got fired? Probably not. But the job wasn't what mattered most in this moment. What mattered was the thought of a future without her stomach clenching. She imagined what these mountains would look like under a blanket of snow. She imagined the boys building up the firepit and spending time together at nights. Someday. It wouldn't happen overnight. Maybe it wouldn't happen at all, but she could still hope.

The engine sounds on the four-wheeler were way too throaty and loud, and she laughed because Kamp and Rhett must have obviously done some upgrades. Their trucks were loud, too. Jacked-up and rowdy, and it was yet another thing that reminded her of Damon's Mountains. These were her kinds of people.

As she revved the engine, Kamp's front door swung open. His green and gold eyes went straight to her, and she froze under his smile. He looked like the happiest man just to see her. Never in her life had any man looked at her like this. Like she was the first thing he wanted to see in the morning to give him the best day.

"You look feral," he said, allowing his door to bang close as he jogged down the steps.

"Thanks. I think," she murmured.

He walked like a man who had utter confidence in

himself with just the right amount of hitch in his walk. His work boots sunk into the soft ground an inch, his threadbare jeans clung to him just right, his white T-shirt hugged his muscular torso, and the flannel shirt he wore flapped behind him in the breeze. He'd rolled up the sleeves, exposing his forearms. Hot, hot, double hot.

He lifted the sack lunch she'd snuck just inside his door this morning. "You're going to spoil me."

"Good. Then you won't leave me."

Kamp didn't miss a beat, just sang, "That's the girl I'll never leave, she's the only one for me, she's a cut above, that girl I love, the only one to set me free." Sure, it was the lyrics from her favorite Beck Brothers song, but Kamp had said "love," and to her, it counted. His singing voice was deep and steady and right on tune. She bet he could belt it if he wanted.

"You think I look feral?" she asked softly, letting the engine of the four-wheeler idle.

"I almost said beautiful, but that didn't seem like a big enough word. Your hair's wild this morning." He caught a strand of a bleach-blond tress and rubbed his thumb down it.

She'd showered last night and let it dry natural.

Kagan had always liked her perfect with tame curls, or straightened with an iron, but today she felt like letting her hair be however it wanted.

"And I can see your spots," he murmured, studying her freckles, his lips curved up just slightly at the corners as he brushed a knuckle across her cheek. "And your eyes have that dark makeup. It makes the green look even brighter."

She caught his hand as he moved to take it away. She pressed her cheek against his palm. "I don't feel feral. My bear feels...happy. I don't know why my eyes are too bright right now."

"Not too bright. Not too anything. You're perfect. I've never seen a more striking woman than you."

Swoon.

"I want to take you back inside and bend you over my bed."

Double swoon.

"Tonight I want to cook for you."

Triple swoon!!

"Cook what?" she asked.

His smile spread across his face slowly. "Barbecue."

Remi gasped and sat up straight on the ATV. "You

mean a Crew dinner? Like I wanted?"

He nodded. "You have me thinking a lot about the changes we need to make around here. And even though Rhett and Grim are fighting it? I bet you're in their heads, too."

"Well, not enough, because they aren't out here and it's 7:02."

"Good. You get to go grizzly on 'em. Do you want to pick up groceries for tonight or wait until I'm off and we can go together?"

"Oooh," she purred, "A grocery store date? You're trying to get in my panties again aren't you?"

Kamp snorted. "Always."

He dug his wallet out of his back pocket, but she stilled his hand. "I've got this."

"No. I don't want you to have to pay for a meal I offered to make."

"Oh, you're still paying. I just plan on stealing it from your cash stash under your mattress."

"What cash stash?"

"The one Rhett's been secretly building."

"Rat!" Rhett called from his porch. When had he snuck out here? "I hear a rat."

"He hides all the mail in one of the drawers in

1010, too," she told Kamp with a shrug. She would spill every damn secret they had if it meant they would get to know each other better.

"I'm still stuck on the cash part," Kamp said. "What the hell, man? You've been in my den? Are you the one who keeps setting the mouse traps for me to find in the middle of the night?"

"You're the worst friend in the world," Rhett yelled at Remi.

"He also plays guitar."

"Oh, I know that," Kamp said. "Rhett's famous."

"Wait, what?"

"And second worst friend in the world goes to you, you nut-sharting cock flea," Rhett said, blasting against his shoulder as he tromped off into the woods.

"Cock flea?" Kamp asked.

"Where's the lunch I made you?" Remi called after him.

"I'd rather eat rabbit shit! See you in an hour when I quit my shift extra early because I don't obey traitor rats!"

"My bear will be waiting for you!" Remi yelled.

Crossing her arms over her chest, she frowned up

at Kamp, but his lips were pursed. He wouldn't look her in the face.

"Why are you laughing? It's not funny."

"He really just called me a cock flea. Look...bright side, Rhett is up almost on time and headed to his machine. You've got two out of three off to work."

"Yeah, and where's the mighty Alpha?"

Kamp's face darkened, and he turned away. "The Reaper is in the woods."

"How do you know?"

Right before he disappeared into the trees, Kamp said, "Because he was up all night fighting."

And then it hit her. His gate wasn't hitched from confidence. Kamp had been hurt. She inhaled quickly and caught the scent, just over the smell of his cologne—the lingering, faint trace of blood. He must've bandaged up his wounds and hidden the smell.

He hid pain better than anyone she'd ever known.

Fucking Grim.

With a growl, she changed the gears on the ATV and gunned it out of the clearing. She mother-effing dared him to jump out of the woods and attack her right now. "Gettin' on my damn nerves," she muttered.

There was a trail that was close to overgrown but still drivable that led down the mountain. She'd even frozen a bag of marbles in the freezer last night to dump on any of the boys who didn't wake up in time. Escaping from frozen marbles was impossible to do. She knew because it's how her brother, Weston, used to wake her up when she was running late for school. If she was honest, a little part of her had been excited about the prospect of dumping them on one of the boys. But Grim was off gallivanting in the woods at the crack of dawn like Count Psychopotamus and she was left worrying about the new injuries Kamp was hiding and wishing she could avenge him.

This quad could move. She changed gears and hit the gas. The wind was cold against her cheeks, but the bite wasn't uncomfortable. It woke her up. She cut to the left with the trail, then back to the right, her back tires skidding across the soft ground. Okay, she was getting the feel of this thing now. How long had it been since she'd ridden one of these? She'd forgotten how fun it was. How free she felt testing how fast a machine could go, how well it could maneuver. Before she knew it, her cheeks were hurting, but still not from the sting of the cold. It was from the giant grin plastered to her face.

Up ahead was the main road, and she zoomed down a steep incline and hit the brakes hard, skidding to the side and rocking to a stop right beside the mailbox. "Whooo!" she yelled, her happy voice echoing through the mountains.

Heart pounding, she dismounted and grabbed the stack of mail that was shoved into the box. There were four identical letters that were hanging out, and the top one had her name on it.

What the heck?

Remi set the pile of mail onto the seat of the ATV and ripped into the one addressed to her.

It was a check for $952. The address was some corporation in New York, but when she read the messy cursive signature, chills blasted up the back of her neck. To anyone else, it would be unreadable, but she'd grown up with this reclusive dragon.

Vyr Daye.

The son of Damon Daye had written her a check.

There was a piece of folded notebook paper behind the check, and with trembling hands, she opened it and read it out loud.

"Dear Remi,

Here is your first paycheck. I hope it is the first of many. These are my mountains, though I don't publicly claim them. I want Grim to be who I know he can be. Who Beaston says he can be. Kamp and Rhett, too. I've been patient as I watch them flounder. Watch them fail. I've been waiting for your father to give me the go-ahead to push them. It's time. You're the push. Bring them in line, Remi. Make them want to live again. Give them purpose. Bind them to my mountains and find happiness and purpose for yourself. I always knew you were special. From the time I was little, that first time Beaston brought you to my father's house, this tiny infant screeching at the top of her lungs, the little grizzly in you growling, it was such a profound memory for me. Your father looked at you like you were the world. I was perhaps seven when he told me for the first time of your destiny and the part I would play in it. We were bound from childhood. I just couldn't see things clearly until I found my own mate. I hope you find yours. Save them.

-Vyr

p.s. If you would like me to kill Kagan, and/or

drain his bank accounts, have him fired from his job, burn him and devour his ashes, or just break both of his knee caps, just say the word. Nox, Torren, and I have been looking for an adventure. Fuck him. It's time for your metamorphosis, Novak Butterfly."

Blinking back tears, she read it again, silently this time. All the puzzle pieces seemed to be falling into place.

It was pointless to call her father and ask what he was up to. He would reveal his plans in his own time. It was his way. Whatever vision he'd seen had convinced him she needed to be here, even from when she was a child. Apparently, he had just been waiting for the right time.

Vyr Daye. The Red Dragon himself. He was the keeper of these mountains? A tear slid down her cheek, clung to her jawline for just a moment before it fell to the gravel road with a soft splat. With every day that passed, all things seemed to point to this beautiful place. To Kamp. To Grim and Rhett.

If Vyr was boss here, then Remi really needed to motivate the lion Crew. Or Pride. Or whatever they were. These would be Vyr's first mountains for logging. And he'd been through Hell. He'd been the brunt of a shifter witch hunt that got his dragon temporarily and painfully ripped from him. But he'd come back to lead his own Crew and their mates so well. She'd been so proud of him, and here he was expanding. Taking this last chance Crew and giving them another shot at a good life.

She sagged onto the seat of the ATV, right on top of the pile of mail like a momma chicken on her eggs, and she cried. She cried for everything. For the person Kagan had made her into, for the loss of herself for those years, for the loss of her stability in the city. She cried for the pain her bear had endured from her decisions, and she cried for how much her father really cared for her. Beaston was the best dad in the whole world.

She cried for Vyr's triumph in not only being here and keeping his volatile dragon in line, but for being big-hearted enough to give other broken shifters a chance.

She cried because she was the only one who saw how truly broken this lion Crew was. She cried for how much pain they must've endured to end up here, and she cried for Kamp's refusal to be bitter after the hand he'd been dealt.

Here...she felt *everything*.

She'd never been meant for the city.

All this time, she'd been destined for mountains.

FIFTEEN

I'm gonna forfeit my man-card and tell you something mushy. Ready?

Remi grinned down at the text from Kamp and responded. *I'm super ready. Mush me.* Send.

I miss you.

Awwwwww! Butterfly emoji, butterfly emoji. Send

I'm so damn ready to finish this lane and head home so I can see you. I'm on lunch. Rhett took his lunch at the same time and sat right next to me. Right. Next. To. Me. He's watching me eat. And also write you this text. He says I need to send you a dick pic.

Tell Rhett he is a genius. And that I will be a better friend. Send.

He says you're a liar, but he likes that about you.

Also his stomach just growled, and he said he should've brought the lunch you made him. Then he stole half of my sandwich. I think I'm on a date with Rhett. He just saw I typed that and said, "Fuck you, cockroach." I guess I've upgraded from cock flea. I think we are becoming friends.

Remi was cracking up outside of the grocery store. *I'm going to buy party supplies. I'll be home soon. Work hard, hit numbers. I have something so cool to tell you tonight about who owns these mountains.* Send.

I love that you just called it home.

Huh. She *had* called it that. Strange.

This was the smallest town she'd ever been in, but she'd looked at every shop on the main street and was totally falling in love with it. Bakery, general store, hardware store, pottery and painting store, grocery store, antiques store, boutique, and right where she parked was a salon.

A salon. She stared at the sign that read *Getchur Hair Did* and then looked at the address in white lettering on the door. 1010 Main Street.

She huffed a laugh and shook her head. Okay, time to go back to her roots. Literally.

Remi poured out of Rhett's truck because, hell yeah, she'd stolen it again and made her way into the salon to see if they had any walk-in appointments available.

****

One hour.

One hour in a chair with hair dye slathered on her tresses, and she looked completely different. Not in a bad way. Remi caught her reflection in the rearview mirror and grinned. This was her natural color. Mom would be happy. She'd always loved that Remi and her sisters had black hair like hers. Her grizzly had come from her father, but this hair, dark as raven feathers, was all Mom's. And Remi's.

She strong-armed all the bags of groceries up the trail toward the trailer park, and when she made it to the clearing, Grim was there, carving something with a knife on his front porch. His face and neck looked awful, all clawed up and angry looking, but he had less venom in his bright gold eyes than he had the last time they'd spoken.

He glared down at the grocery bags she was toting but then went back to carving. When she reached Kamp's front door, he asked, "Is that all the groceries?"

"I have one more trip."

Silently, Grim stood and made his way to the trail that led to the parking lot.

Stunned, Remi blinked hard as he disappeared into the trees. "Okay then." He might've been headed to burn the truck, purchase a voodoo doll of her, or walk out of here forever for all she knew, but she got the feeling he was planning to help. That was nice of the monster. She let herself into Kamp's den and unloaded the bags, and when she came back out, she found the rest of the bags on the front porch and Grim setting up the Cornhole game she'd bought on clearance for half off.

"You hurt Kamp last night," she said.

Grim straightened his spine and lifted his chin. The claw marks on his cheek looked so painful. "So?" he asked.

"So someday, I hope you get the Reaper under control."

"Why do you care?"

"For lots of reasons. But Kamp is the biggest one. He's good, Grim."

"You know what the Tarian Pride always teaches

dominants?"

Remi shook her head slowly.

"To kill the weak."

Remi gestured to Grim's clawed-up face and neck. "He doesn't look weak to me."

A flash of something she didn't understand roiled in his eyes. "I wasn't talking about him."

A branch snapped, and out stepped Kamp from the woods. The instant he saw Remi, his smile lit up the evening. God, it was good to see him. Something that had tightened up in her chest throughout the day now loosened, and she exhaled the tension she hadn't even realized she was carrying. He strode right to her and lifted her up off the ground, hugged her so tightly the rest of the world disappeared. Suddenly, it was just her and Kamp, spinning slowly, her arms wrapped around his neck, his arms wrapped around her waist.

She loved this. This man made her feel safe with a touch, and it was a first-and-only for her. Cupping his cheeks, she searched his gold and green mismatched eyes. Special man, wiggling his way into a hardened heart.

"I like your hair like this." His attention drifted

down from the top of her hair to the ends curling near her breasts. "The dark suits you."

"This is my natural color," she whispered, her cheeks heating under his sweet attention.

"How does it make you feel?"

"Like my old self. The parts I liked."

"Mmmm, good. Now, what am I cooking for you tonight, hotgirl?" he murmured.

"Steak and baked potatoes," she hummed happily.

"Atta girl, good choice."

"And I got Cornhole!"

"I saw." He looked at the two angled pallets Grim had set up several yards apart. "Two important questions. Did you get bean bags to throw, and are we turning it into a drinking game?"

Remi laughed before she answered, "Hell yes and also hell yes."

He chuckled and twitched his head back toward the darkening woods. "Rhett is almost done. He's loading up the truck with the logs we cut today. We have to take it to the lumber yard in the morning. First load we've had ready in a week."

Proud down to her marrow, she kissed him, let her lips linger there, and then pulled back. "How does it make you feel?" she asked, repeating his question.

"Really fuckin' good, like my old self." Leaning in, he nipped her neck. "Come on, I need to get the grill warmed up."

Remi scanned the clearing to ask Grim how he liked his steak cooked, but the Alpha was gone. Just…vanished.

"He does that," Kamp murmured, frowning at the woods. He settled her onto her feet, slid his big strong hand around hers, then led her toward the bags on his front porch, but she squeezed his hand and tugged him to a stop. His calloused palm was so warm.

"Are you okay?" he asked.

"Kamp, look," she whispered holding up their hands. "You like touching me."

Was that a blush on his chiseled cheeks? It was hard to tell because the sun was setting behind the mountains and casting everything in evening shadows. But…it looked like his cheeks were turning red.

"You're special, Remi," he said. "Before you came along, all I could think about was my son and what I lost. It was like an endless loop in my head, and with my animal, that made it impossible to cope. But from the second you showed up, I didn't feel alone. You came charging at me, this big beautiful silver grizzly bear, and my animal just stopped the loop. He's been staring at you ever since. My son will always be in my head, but you give me rest. You are a fixer. Has anyone told you that?"

"No."

"You're this light, and you come into a dark room and change the makeup of everything in it. Whether it wants to be changed or not."

"Do you want to be changed?"

"Only by you."

She ducked her head to hide her mushy smile. "I have an admission."

"I'm ready," he murmured, tucking a flyaway lock of her newly darkened hair behind her ear.

"You scare me more than anyone has ever scared me."

Kamp hooked a finger under her chin and lifted her gaze to his. "Why?"

"Because you feel important, and I have this feeling that when you get tired of me and throw me away, I won't be able to recover. Everything keeps pointing to me staying here with you. All these little signs. It feels like all my life, every decision I've made, has been a puzzle piece. And before now, I couldn't figure out how to put them all together. And when I'm around you, all the pieces seem to match up."

"You're waiting for the other shoe to drop?"

Remi bit her bottom lip to punish her emotions and nodded.

"What did he do to you?"

"Who?"

"The asshole who threw you away?"

"He just got bored." Remi shrugged. "I think that's the part that bothers me the most. That I'm so leave-able. That I'm so expendable. Unlovable. He stopped saying he loved me six months before he left. He stopped touching me, stopped sleeping with me, stopped telling me anything kind. So I worked harder to make him happy, to get us back to where we were, to make him love me again. But the more of myself I sacrificed, the less he cared. And by the end, I didn't even know myself anymore."

"It's not a man's job to make you work for his love. It's his job to care for you as you are and never make you question your place in his life. Your ex wasn't a man. He was an unworthy boy, and he wasn't your mate."

"But what if you aren't either?" she whispered before she could change her mind.

His gold eye flashed bright. "In a month you won't question that anymore. I'll be understanding because you were just burned, but you'll stop questioning if I want you by my side. Just as you are. No sacrificing yourself, just be your badass, independent, ATV-ripping, truck-thieving, mouthy, beautiful-soul self. You'll see how addicted you got me. I wish you could spend a second in my head. One second, and you would feel my lion just staring at you in wonder."

She giggled. "I'm a mess, I have hair dye on my forehead, I cried a little today so my makeup is all smeared, the lady at the salon found two leaves in my hair from all the ATV-ripping, *and* I bought you a silly present, but I'm too embarrassed to give it to you."

He grinned. "You got me a present?"

"Yes! It's a beer pong table. I want to put the Pen15 Juice logo on it. I kind of got it for the whole Crew, but mostly for you."

He shook his head like he didn't understand, so she explained. "You'll be steady if you have a Crew. I can't fix what went wrong with your custody of your son or the bad time you went through before I came along. But I can try to give your life balance and make it happy now. Rhett and Grim play a part in that. So…beer pong. For bonding."

His eyes were huge as her words tumbled end over end. He blinked slowly. "Okaaay. And Cornhole," he said, looking over at the bean-bag tossing game in front of the trailers.

"Yes! And I'll keep getting us fun shit until everyone can go a day without bleeding each other. I'm not even asking you three to get along. Just…stop hating each other so we can turn this mountain into the most productive motherfuckin' logging mountain in the world! I know the numbers they put up in Damon's Mountains. I want us to give the Gray Backs and the Boarlanders and the Ashe Crew some competition!"

"Woman, we just finished our first day of actual work, and Grim didn't even show up for the shift. Those are some big goals to put on a trio of utter fuck-ups."

"Well, that's what I want, and I'm pretty determined to get there. Even if it takes us fifty years."

"And it will. Fifty years. Because we are literally the shittiest Crew I've ever heard of."

Remi pointed her finger to the sky and exclaimed, "Not anymore! You have child support to pay, beer to make, and logs to chop like a sexy, bitey, scratchy Paul Bunyan."

"Paul Bunyan had a lucky blue ox."

"And you have a lucky Novak Grizzly. Yes, I'm full of myself today. You may rub my boobs for good luck if you want."

Eyes dancing, he put both hands on her boobs and squeezed.

"Feel that, Kamp? That's luck flowing from my teets into your hands."

"Mostly I feel my dick getting hard."

"Lucky," she whispered.

He snorted and burst out laughing, then dragged her against him and hugged her up tight. "You're going to ruin this Crew's plans, aren't you?"

"What plans? To fail and suck and eventually kill each other off? Yes. Fuck that plan. I have new plans for you."

"Okay, I'll play beer pong and Cornhole and push

the Crew in the field if you do one thing for me."

"Anything. Except anal. That's an exit-only hole for me. Sorry, dirty boy."

"Oh my God, not what I was going to ask at all in any way."

She grinned brightly. "Bored of me yet?"

"That's the compromise. I'll work on my baggage if you work on yours. No questioning if I'm going to leave or if you're unlovable. You aren't leave-able, Remi. You gotta turn your head around on that stuff. Deal?"

She leaned forward, rested her forehead on his chest, and sighed. Kamp didn't realize it, but he was a fixer, too. It was going to be hard letting go of all the things she'd been taught over the last few years, but Kamp was right. She couldn't just ask him to fix his shit without working on hers. And she loved that he cared enough to want better for her.

So now the hard part began.

"Deal," she whispered.

SIXTEEN

Remi slid the metal spatula under the hamburger patty and flipped it. The air was getting colder with every week that passed, and their barbecue days were numbered. The snow would hit these mountains in a month. But for now, evenings suited her warm-natured bear just fine. The boys seemed good, too, if their T-shirts and holey-kneed jeans were anything to go by.

She hoped they got back soon. The burgers were almost done, and the homemade French fries she'd made were sitting in a covered bowl waiting to be devoured already. They were getting cold. The Crew was unloading a truck of lumber at the lumberyard a couple mountains over. Usually, it didn't take them this long to return, though.

She was hoping tonight's barbecue went better than the others.

The first one, Kamp and Rhett tried to play Cornhole, but Rhett got pissed at losing, Changed into a lion, and during a huge Crew fight, they broke one of the Cornhole boards. Remi had left her grilling station where she was supposed to be flipping the steaks to break up the fight, but Rhett clawed her, so she punched him in his stupid lion face, which hurt her hand, and then Kamp latched onto his throat to defend Remi and nearly killed him. When she finally got them Changed back and out of murder-mode, she returned to the grill to find the steaks burnt to a crispy-crisp, and the only thing that was edible was the macaroni and cheese she'd made. Grim showed up just in time for dinner and chewed on one of the burnt steaks while he stared at them, unspeaking. And when Remi had tried to play twenty questions so everyone could get to know each other better, Rhett only answered with perverted words, Grim had answered "pass" to every question, and Kamp closed up like the little violent, ornery, standoffish clam he was with the boys.

Progress on the first barbecue: 0%.

The second week, it went a little better. No one broke the newly duct-taped Cornhole game. Kamp made some hella delicious ribs that weren't burnt to ashes, and Remi had braved bringing out the new beer pong table.

Kamp and Grim had made it through three tosses of their ping-pong balls before they Changed and got in a fight that dragged out to the woods. Used to their shenanigans now, Remi had shot-gunned a beer and sank into one of the plastic lawn chairs beside Rhett, who was scrolling on his phone as if he couldn't care less that his Crew was out in the woods trying to kill each other.

But the ribs had tasted delicious.

So…progress on the second barbecue: 4%.

This week, Remi was bound and determined to make this barbecue the best yet. Why? Because they had big reasons to celebrate.

One, all three boys had finished a shift, even Grim. And yes, he probably did it just to avoid her pestering and frozen marbles and the early morning call from Vyr that had made his face go pale, but it counted.

Two, with Juno's help, she'd gotten a moving

company to pack up her belongings in the city and ship it all to the mountains.

Three, she'd come up with a Crew name she was pretty sure the boys would approve of. And no, it wasn't the Penis Juice Crew, as Rhett kept suggesting.

Four, she'd slept over at Kamp's place three nights in a row so he hadn't Changed or fought the Reaper since Wednesday.

Five, this morning her dad had messaged her four words that had filled her heart and pushed out any lingering disdain she had for herself. *I'm proud of you.*

Six, it was hamburger night. She freaking loved hamburger night, and hamburgers deserved their own celebration day.

Seven...she couldn't remember being happier than she was here. Sure, the boys were a mess, and they fought all the time. They were crass and rude. She wanted to turn grizzly and maim them at least three times a day, but as time went on, she'd opened up here. She'd begun to trust.

A month ago, she'd been so ready to hate men for the rest of her life. She'd been prepared to be bitter forever and never trust anyone with her heart again. And then she'd met Kamp, and he had opened her eyes and heart. And then Grim and Rhett had surprised her, too. It was a different relationship. It was fighting and clawing and debating every single sentence, but if one of them pushed her too far, you bet your ass the other two lit him up. They were protective of her in their own ways, and she knew that if push came to shove, they would have her back, even if she was wrong. They would aim that horrid behavior at anyone who ever tried to hurt her.

With this rag-tag Crew of monsters…she was really safe.

The rumble of an eighteen-wheeler engine was the most beautiful sound in the world to her. It meant Kamp was home. It meant the hollow chasm that sat in her chest when he was too far away closed up again. It meant that in just a few minutes, she would be whole.

The burgers were done, so she took them off the grill, one by one, put them onto a plate and covered it up. She'd meant to sit on Kamp's front porch stairs to wait for him so they could have their moment when he came up the trail, always ahead of the others so he could see her sooner. It was their tradition now. But her phone dinged, and when she checked it, the message read, *Swear to me on your life that you'll keep him safe.*

Remi frowned at the unfamiliar number and typed, *Who is this?* Send.

I know who you are now. Todd told me about your family. About the Crew you grew up in, the Gray Backs. About how protective your kind are. I need your word that you'll keep my boy safe when he's there.

Remi sat straight up, her heart pounding out of her chest. *Yes, I swear no harm will come to him. Raider has my fealty. But more than that, he'll have the protection of his father. Kamp would never let anything happen to him. That boy is his world.*

That's what I needed to hear before I do this.

Hope blossoming in her chest, she typed out, *Do what?* with shaking hands. Send.

The eighteen-wheeler was on the backside of the trailer park, up a narrow trail near where the boys had been clearing timber, and the engine cut off. They were home.

She stood, heart drumming in her chest, but as she began to run for Kamp, she saw a large, stoic figure standing there, right on the edge of the woods.

His bright green eyes were glowing in the

evening shadows. “Dad?” she whispered.

Beaston Novak stepped out from under a towering pine and a slow smile stretched his whiskered face. Growing up, she’d always thought he was the strongest man in the whole world. Now, as a grown woman, she still thought the same. His shoulders were just as wide, his eyes still as deep and holding a thousand secrets. His hair had silvered at the temples over the years, the same shade of his grizzly’s fur. His eyes wrinkled at the corners when he smiled at her.

It was so damn good to see him. Relief pooled in her veins as she walked toward him, matching his pace. But the last few steps she ran and launched herself at him. He caught her easy, because this had been their routine from the time she could walk. His bear felt monstrous, so big he took up the whole forest, but to Remi, he wasn’t scary. His bear had kept her safe all those years.

“Remi, not much time. Tell me. Does he make sense to you now?”

“What?” she asked, her chin resting on his shoulder.

“Kamp. Does he make sense to your heart?”

Dad, in his own way, was asking if she loved Kamp. She wasn't able to answer. The single word "yes" didn't seem big enough to match the depth of her feelings. She'd never felt happiness like this, like she did with Kamp. All she could do was nod her head, digging her chin into his shoulder so he would understand.

"Something is about to happen," he murmured. "I want to be here. See your face. See Kamp's."

"I don't understand," she murmured.

Kamp stepped through the trees behind her father, trailed by Grim and Rhett. Dad had to have known the lions were here, but he didn't tense up like he would've with any other predator at his back. Instead, the tension in his shoulders eased.

He set her on her feet and turned slowly, placing her in front of him for the first time in her life. He'd always put her behind him protectively. "Kamp Bryant Nichols," Dad rumbled.

Kamp's lightened gold and green eyes drifted from Dad to Remi and back. He nodded his chin in respect. "Beaston Novak. It's an honor to meet you."

"I've watched you since you were a cub," Dad told him, gripping Remi's shoulders from behind.

Kamp's eyes went wide. "Why?"

"Your fate takes jobs. It took mine."

"What job?"

"To protect my little bear." Her dad gently nudged Remi forward.

Heart beating out of her throat with shock and happiness, she padded across the blanket of pine needles toward Kamp. Without hesitation, she slid her hands around his waist and melted into his open arms.

Remi arched her face back to watch the slow smile stretch Kamp's face.

He said to her father, "If that is my fate, it's the best fate I could've wished for."

Oh, what those words did to her. He was really hers. Meant to be hers, meant to be by her side for always. She'd waited her whole life just to know for sure that she was coveted, just to covet the mate who was meant for her. She'd finally got it right.

Grim and Rhett flanked Kamp and both nodded respectfully, murmured Beaston's name low. Their eyes were so bright, they were hard to look at.

"You haven't been a Crew," Beaston said. "I've been watching. Change it. From today, you have to change it. My girl will be a mother after today. Kamp will be a father. You will have a cub in the Crew."

"What do you mean?" Kamp asked, his body going rigid.

"I came here to see your face when it happened."

"I don't understand what's happening," Grim said, his voice more snarl than human.

Beaston gestured to Remi. "It was my job to have you. My first bear cub. Oldest bear cub. Weston was my raven boy, and you were my little bear. When your momma handed you to me, I was afraid to break you. I thought I would be bad at girl cubs. I thought you would be too fragile and I would hurt you. But I was the fragile one with you. It was my Ana's job to have you, too. All special fates. I watched Kamp. Watched him from a boy because I saw him for my girl. I wanted to watch him grow up because someday he would be mine, too. My only lion boy. I have to trust him to take care of you. And the rest of the Rogue Pride Crew.

Remi gasped. "That's the name I thought of."

"Rogue Pride?" Grim asked.

Remi turned to them. "You're all rogue lions, who haven't figured out that you are a pride yet. Who haven't figured out you are a Crew."

Rhett chimed in, "I still vote for—"

"Don't you even fuckin' say Penis Juice again," Grim growled.

Rhett stuck his bottom lip out and then whispered, "But it's my favorite word combination."

Remi pursed her lips against a smile and then cleared her throat. "Dad, this is my Crew. Rogue Pride. This is Grim and Rhett. And my Kamp."

Dad nodded to each of them and then stepped to the side. He pointed to the trailer park. "He's here."

"Who's here?" Kamp asked.

"The Prince of Rogue Pride. The one who will be raised by monsters. The one who will change everything for lions when the Big War comes. Blood-and-bone of Kamp, boy-of-the-heart to the Novak Grizzly, raised in the ways of the Saga Pride, ward of the Reaper." Beaston thumped himself in the chest. "And grandson-of-the-heart to me."

Kamp swallowed audibly. "Raider?"

Beaston nodded.

"Hello?" a woman's voice echoed through the clearing.

"That's Sophia," Kamp whispered. "That's

Sophia," he repeated louder, grabbing Remi's hand.

She ran behind him as he bolted for the trailer park. The second they rounded 1010, Kamp locked his powerful legs and came to a stop so abruptly, Remi ran into his back.

In the clearing in front of the trailers stood Sophia, head held high, her soft brown eyes on Kamp. Clutching her hand was Raider, his eyes bright green and gold and studying on Kamp. He wore little jean shorts and a blue backpack.

"Raider," Kamp uttered, striding forward.

The second Kamp released Remi's hand, she put her palm over her mouth to hide her lips trembling. Her eyes burned as her mate went slowly to his knees in front of his son. Even now, he towered over the small boy.

"I'm…" Kamp swallowed hard and shook his head. "I'm your…"

Raider looked up at his mom and then back to Kamp. "I know you." He dug in his pocket and pulled out a locket in the shape of a book. He pried it open with his little fingers and shoved it toward Kamp.

Inside was a picture of Kamp's smiling profile.

Kamp expelled a breath and his shoulders sagged.

Remi couldn't look at his face right now or she would lose the battle with the tears welling up in her eyes.

"Can I hug you?" he asked. He looked up at Sophia. "Can I hug him?"

Two tears streaked down Sophia's face and she sniffed, then nodded.

Raider moved first. He wrapped his little arms around Kamp's neck, and Kamp pulled him into his lap, held him close, and rocked him. "I never thought I would get to see you."

"I'll be back to get him tomorrow morning," Sophia said thickly, turning on her heel. Her shoulders were shaking as she made her way to the trail that led to the parking lot.

Raider watched her go, his eyes round as saucers. Everyone watched her leave. Only Kamp spoke. "Sophia! Thank you."

Remi stood there with her hands over her mouth, completely shocked with what was happening.

"You get to stay with me?" Kamp asked.

Shyly, Raider nodded. "Mommy said you'll help me be a good lion so it doesn't hurt so bad."

"Okay." Kamp looked around at the Crew and back to his son. "Okay," he repeated. "Are you hungry?"

Raider nodded. Were his eyes somehow getting bigger? He looked like a cute little wood sprite if she ignored the growl that rattled his throat.

Remi stepped forward and knelt down beside them. "Hi, Raider."

"I remember you."

"Wait, you know her, too?" Kamp asked.

"Yeah, she was at Mommy's flower shop. Is that a game?" he asked, pointing to the taped-up Cornhole boards.

"Yeah, do you want to play?" Rhett asked.

Grim now stood next to Beaston, right on the edge of the trees, his arms crossed over his chest. They were talking too low for Remi to hear, and then both retreated into the woods and disappeared like fog.

Raider handed Kamp his backpack and bolted for Rhett, who tossed him a beanbag. Raider missed it, and the giggle that bubbled up from him changed the makeup of the mountains. That sound... Remi couldn't fully explain the impact it had on her soul. Like she'd been waiting her whole life to hear that little laugh. Her bear was quiet and watchful, practically purring when the boy got close to throwing the beanbag in the hole on the first try.

Beside her, Kamp helped her to her feet and asked, "Did you do this for me?"

"I went to see Sophia when I left. I had this plan to go back to the city afterward, but I wanted to fix your life before I disappeared from it. I wanted to give you a shot at happiness." Her voice broke on the last word.

Kamp nodded over and over, his eyes roiling with emotion. He cupped her cheeks. "I love you, Remi Novak. You know that, right?"

A soft sob left her lips. She gripped his wrists, nuzzled her cheek against his hand. "I love you, too."

He pressed his lips to hers, let them linger there before he eased away. A smile illuminated his face right before he called out to Rhett and Raider, "Do you two want to play doubles?"

With Remi tight against his side, one arm draped around her shoulders and his cub's little blue backpack dangling from his fist, he led them toward the others.

And as she watched Kamp teach Raider how to toss a beanbag, she knew it was time.

He'd asked her once to choose a moment when she was proud of him and wanted to ask for his claiming mark. She would never forget this moment, watching her mate beside his boy. Feeling his happiness, watching his easy smile, hearing his deep laughter intermixed with Raider's giggles.

Her father had asked her if Kamp made sense to her, and she'd only nodded because she hadn't been able to find words big enough to answer.

She'd been in a wide, dark hole when she had shown up here, desperate to distract herself from her own pain. And she'd found medicine. She'd found Kamp. She'd found a balm to her aching soul. He made her feel like more than enough. He'd given her a Crew. And yeah, they were a mess, all broken in their own ways. They were a Crew of old rusted blades, their edges all chipped and jagged, but they worked. He was giving her a boy-of-the-heart, as her father had put it. She had purpose here, a drive, a happy future. Kamp had given her a place. He'd given her a home. 1010. Trust. Love. Devotion.

The only thing he hadn't given her was a claiming mark.

As Rhett took a turn, Kamp's attention arched to

her. Standing next to his cub, he gave her the biggest, happiest grin she'd ever seen on his face.

"I'm ready," she murmured just loud enough for him to hear.

Ready to be claimed, ready to be paired up, ready to grow her roots deep, right here in these mountains with the man she loved.

Oh, he knew exactly what she meant. She could tell in the way his smile changed. How it softened. He looked at her like she was the most beautiful thing he'd ever seen. Her—with all of her imperfections and baggage. She'd found the man who appreciated all of her.

This man not only made sense to her.

He made her whole life make sense.

EPILOGUE

Kamp looked down at the dead bunny on his front porch and sighed. Fucking Reaper wouldn't stop leaving them here. He only did it on the weekend's Kamp and Remi had visitation with Raider, so he was pretty sure the psycho was bringing his son presents, in his own slightly disturbing way.

Rhett was striding right for him, and Kamp viciously fought the urge to step back inside and close the door. It was too early for whatever Rhett was holding in his hand.

"I've brought a gift for the lad," he said grandly.

Kamp bit back a sigh. "Why does that box have air holes?"

"Because I spied on you one time and heard Remi

say mice are lucky, so I got a pet for Raider."

"You got him a mouse?" Kamp whispered, trying not to tip off his son and Remi, who were eating breakfast inside.

"No. I got him something even better." Rhett took the stairs two at a time and shoved the cardboard box into Kamp's chest. The sound of scratching claws sounded from inside. Great.

Kamp opened one of the flaps carefully and gritted his teeth at what he found. Inside, there was a hideous, little hairless rodent. "Is that a mole rat?"

"Yep. Raider! I got you a pet, man. Come see your new childhood best friend."

"For fuck's sake, Rhett!" Kamp said as Rhett pulled the creature from the box. "Are those even legal to have as pets? Where did you steal it from?"

Rhett cuddled it against his chest. He tried to nuzzle it with his cheek, but it bit him, and Rhett flinched. Served him right. "Never you mind."

"Remi said a nice mouse with giant nuts is lucky. That looks like a female, and she seems rabid."

"Females are the better sex," Rhett said with a shrug as he tried to pet the little bald creature's nose. When it bit him again, he yelped and flinched back.

"Plus, it's funny to have a female pet that looks like a wrinkly dick. Raider-man! Come here!"

"Coming!" came his son's little squeaky voice from inside, followed by the echo of little footsteps.

Kamp was going to kill Rhett. "Remember when I said no pets for him yet?"

"No. You said I couldn't get him a wombat, a golden eagle, or a cobra. You didn't say anything about mole rats."

"I hate you," Kamp muttered just as Raider rushed out the door and past his legs. He was wearing Kamp's yellow hard hat that kept slipping around his head. "Boy, don't touch her. She bites."

"Like every girl," Rhett said with a bright smile as he knelt down to show Raider the little monster.

"What is that?" Remi asked from the open doorway, looking horrified.

"Say hello to...wait, what should we name her?" Rhett asked Raider.

"Waffles with Peanut Butter!"

Okay, Kamp now had to work to hide his smile. Remi had made Raider his favorite waffles smeared with peanut butter for breakfast.

"Good choice, buddy," Kamp said, ruffling his hair.

Rhett flinched his hand back again and whispered, "I want to love her, but she's just so angry."

"Look, Dad, Mr. Reaper brought us another dead rabbit," Raider said, squatting near the poor thing.

"Yeah, that'll be a fun one to explain to your mom," Kamp muttered.

When Waffles with Peanut Butter peed on Rhett, Kamp snorted. Okay, maybe he liked her. The little hellion certainly fit in with the Crew.

Grim walked back with a sack lunch in one hand and a chainsaw in the other, his yellow hard hat already on his head. He slid them all an angry look and said, "Get to work. I have the Red Dragon up my ass about our numbers."

"Huh," he muttered to himself as the Alpha strode off toward the area where they were clearing timber. "I think that's the first time I've ever seen him care about numbers."

Rhett set the mole rat into the box again and handed it to Raider. "Guard her with your life."

As Rhett made his way off the porch and followed Grim to the job site, Remi meandered out with her mug of coffee, kissed his shoulder, and sat in the porch chair right next to where Kamp was standing. She leaned her head against his hip, and he massaged the back of her neck just for the excuse to touch her and settle his animal. The neck of her shirt was all stretched out and exposed the claiming mark he'd given her a few weeks ago. He was so damn proud every time he saw it.

Out of everyone, she'd chosen him. As long as he lived, he would never get over how damn lucky he was.

He brushed his finger across the bite mark, and Remi's response was immediate. Chills rippled up her forearms, and she smiled so sweetly at him. These were his favorite mornings, her dark hair all wild from sleep, her freckles stark against her fair skin, her smile easy. She wielded a powerful animal and was a complete badass, but he and Raider got to see her soft side. The caring, protective, loving side that kept this home a happy one.

She was the glue around here and didn't even realize how necessary she was to his life or this Crew. She was just...herself. Steady, happy, grateful, easy-going, completely loveable, utterly un-leave-able mate.

Kamp pulled the hard hat from his cub's head. "I better get to work."

"I want to go!"

"Ask Remi to bring you up at lunch time, and I'll let you pull the levers on the processor for a while."

The boy hugged his leg, picked up his box of furious animal, and then went to sit in Remi's lap. He was a cuddler and tended to drift to her when he was feeling uncertain about anything. Kamp loved it. Watching Remi with his boy put all his broken pieces back together.

He leaned down and kissed her lips, his grip tight on the back of her neck, kissed the top of Raider's head, and made his way down the stairs.

He looked back when he got to the tree line. Raider and Remi were looking in the box with matching smiles as they chattered on. His world was in that chair, on that porch, in these mountains, in this home.

She caught his eye and kissed her fingertips then waved. God, she was beautiful. And his life was beautiful because of her. All the hardships he'd faced up until now were worth it for moments like these.

Life would never be perfect in the Rogue Pride

Crew.

Not by other people's standards.

Money would always be tight, work would always be hard, the Crew would always fight. They would never be "fixed" completely.

But Remi was teaching Kamp to accept that and appreciate the life he did have for what it was.

He'd come into this last chance Crew hoping to survive it.

But now Kamp wasn't just surviving.

He was really living.

Want more of these characters?

The Daughters of Beasts series is a standalone series set in the Damon's Mountains Universe.
More of these characters can be found in the following series:

Saw Bears

Gray Back Bears

Fire Bears

Boarlander Bears

Harper's Mountains

Kane's Mountains

Red Havoc Panthers

Sons of Beasts

About the Author

T.S. Joyce is devoted to bringing hot shifter romances to readers. Hungry alpha males are her calling card, and the wilder the men, the more she'll make them pour their hearts out. She werebear swears there'll be no swooning heroines in her books. It takes tough-as-nails women to handle her shifters.

She lives in a tiny town, outside of a tiny city, and devotes her life to writing big stories. Foodie, wolf whisperer, ninja, thief of tiny bottles of awesome smelling hotel shampoo, nap connoisseur, movie fanatic, and zombie slayer, and most of this bio is true.

Bear Shifters? Check

Smoldering Alpha Hotness? Double Check

Sexy Scenes? Fasten up your girdles, ladies and gents, it's gonna to be a wild ride.

For more information on T. S. Joyce's work,
visit her website at
www.tsjoyce.com

Printed in Great Britain
by Amazon